"Do you remember anything now?" she whispered.

"No, but I do know one thing. This feels right."

"Well, yes, but...you don't remember me."

"You've been caring and worried and, well...I think I do know you. Somehow, I feel you with me. I see how compassionate you are," he said, taking her head in his hands. His eyes were bright and intense and, goodness, he looked like Risk again, even with the bandage around his head. "And I'm certainly responding to you." He planted a beautiful kiss to her mouth and then paused. "Unless, we haven't done this before? Have we? Tell me we have."

"We've done this before."

"I need you, April. I need the connection."

She absorbed those words, which touched her deep down in her soul. She'd never reacted to any man the way she'd reacted to him. This Risk was sincere, genuine and sweet. This Risk was in need of more than sex, but intimacy, a bridge to his past.

And today, she was it.

* * *

Stranded and Seduced is part of the Boone Brothers of Texas series.

Dear Reader,

Sometimes things happen that change the course of your whole life. For River "Risk" Boone, losing his status as rodeo champ and being dumped by his superstar girlfriend do just that. Now Risk is immersed in the family business at Boone Incorporated— something far less thrilling...until he seeks the expertise of beautiful Realtor April Adams for a new Boone company acquisition. April desperately needs the sale of Canyon Lake Lodge to keep her agency afloat, but she's been personally burned by Risk once before, leaving her disheartened, so she and her friends concoct a fantastic lie to keep Risk from blurring the lines between professionalism and personal attraction.

Add in a vicious Texas storm, two people dedicated to their individual purposes, a remote abandoned lodge, undeniable sexual attraction, and we have ourselves a story!

There's more to this tale than meets the eye, with several twists and turns along the way, but no spoilers here, I promise. Only a read that will hopefully entertain and make you smile, while stirring up deep emotions for two people totally attracted to each other, but not necessarily destined for love.

Until they are.

Happy reading!

Charlene Sands

CHARLENE SANDS

———

STRANDED AND SEDUCED

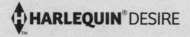

Recycling programs
for this product may
not exist in your area.

ISBN-13: 978-1-335-60386-9

Stranded and Seduced

Printed in U.S.A.

HARLEQUIN®
www.Harlequin.com

Charlene Sands is a *USA TODAY* bestselling author of more than forty romance novels. She writes sensual contemporary romances and stories of the Old West. When not writing, Charlene enjoys sunny Pacific beaches, great coffee, reading books from her favorite authors and spending time with her family. You can find her on Facebook and Twitter, write her at PO Box 4883, West Hills, CA 91308, or sign up for her newsletter for fun blogs and ongoing contests at charlenesands.com.

Books by Charlene Sands

Harlequin Desire

The Slades of Sunset Ranch

Sunset Surrender
Sunset Seduction
The Secret Heir of Sunset Ranch
Redeeming the CEO Cowboy

Heart of Stone

The Texan's Wedding Escape
Heart of a Texan

Boone Brothers of Texas

Texan for the Taking
Stranded and Seduced

Visit her Author Profile page at Harlequin.com, or charlenesands.com, for more titles.

You can find Charlene Sands on Facebook, along with other Harlequin Desire authors, at Facebook.com/harlequindesireauthors.

To my dear friends Mary and Richard.
Your friendship, love and support
mean so much.

Here's to more Palm Springs days
and happy times!

One

April always knew her luck would run out one day.

In a town the size of Boone Springs, she couldn't avoid River "Risk" Boone forever.

But she hadn't expected to see the tall, handsome Texan walk into her real estate agency that morning.

Her stomach in knots, she gazed at him from across her desk. He tipped his hat back, his eyes a mesmerizing dark brown, his skin still as bronzed as it had been in his rodeo days. Wearing crisp jeans and a tan button-down shirt, his business casual attire and good looks turned heads in the Texas town founded by his ancestors. He'd turned her head once, too, and that had been a big mistake.

"Hello, April."

The deep timbre of his voice, the way he drawled

her name, gentle and sure, rang in her ears. On wobbly legs she rose from her desk. "Risk, w-what are you doing here?"

His brows arched as he looked her over from head to toe, a gleam in his eyes as if he was remembering the night they'd shared. Heat rose up her throat, and she was stunned Risk still had the ability to jumble her thoughts.

Clovie, her assistant and good friend, gave her a quizzical look from the desk adjacent to hers. Clovie knew something about her past history with him.

"I'm here on Boone business. I understand you've spoken with my brother Mason's secretary about the Canyon Lake property."

"Yes, that's correct. I answered some of her questions about the lodge. But that's as far as it went. I, uh, do we have an appointment?"

She knew darn well they didn't. And she also knew darn well she wasn't going to turn him away on some false premise that he needed to make one. She didn't know why she'd asked that question, other than a bad case of nerves. It's not as if she could ignore a member of the Boone family. The three Boone brothers were wealthy cattle ranchers and entrepreneurs. They owned much of the town.

"Never mind," she said. "If you have questions about Canyon Lake Lodge, I can help you."

He gave her a nod. "Apparently you did a great job talking up the lodge, because we're definitely interested in finding out more about—" Risk stopped speaking. Oh God, he'd noticed the pain in her eyes, the frown she couldn't conceal.

Two years ago, they'd spent one night together. She hadn't expected diamonds and flowers afterward, but she had expected him to be there when she woke up in the morning.

"Listen, is there someplace we can talk privately?" Risk asked after a long pause.

Clovie piped up instantly. "I've got the bank deposit ready, April. I was just leaving." She stood, gathering up a folder and hoisting her handbag over her shoulder. "I'll stop for lunch and see you in an hour or so."

"Okay."

Clovie dashed out quickly as both watched her leave and shut the door behind her.

"Ask and ye shall receive." April's sardonic tone shifted Risk's attention back to her. She was at a complete loss. Seeing him stirred up deep feelings of hurt and abandonment again. Mostly she hated that Risk Boone, the ex-rodeo champion, had treated her like one of his buckle bunnies when she'd believed they'd really connected that night in Houston. Though he'd once been her secret high school crush, the fantasy-come-true night they'd shared two years ago had turned into a bad memory.

"April, look, I'm here because you have the listing for Canyon Lake Lodge. I'm the new head of real estate acquisitions for Boone Inc. My brothers want to expand the business and like the idea of opening a lodge. I didn't make an appointment because I wasn't sure you'd see me. I owe you an apology."

"You were afraid I wouldn't want to see you?"

"Judging by the sound of your voice, I'm not far from the mark, am I?"

"Your apology is a little late in coming, wouldn't you say?" She folded her arms across her middle, not in a show of attitude but to help brace herself. "That was quite some time ago."

"I've been working out of town a lot these past few years. It's not an excuse, but simply the truth." He ran his hand through his hair. "Listen, I was in a bad place back then. I couldn't stay. Shannon really messed me up and, well, I wasn't ready for…you. I couldn't give anything back. I guess—no, I know—I ran scared. And I'm sorry."

I wasn't ready for…you.

Oh God, what a silly fool she'd been thinking that talking openly and sharing confidences and making love throughout the night would mean something, when all she'd been to him was a one-night stand.

She'd known about his two-year relationship with superstar actress Shannon Wilkes—the tabloids had made sure the entire country was well versed in the details of their relationship and scandalous breakup. Risk had been a rodeo celebrity at the top of his bronc-busting game, and Shannon had won a Golden Globe. They'd been paired as a super couple, until Risk took a bad fall from a bronc, injuring his shoulder and ending his rodeo career. Shortly after, Shannon broke up with him and immediately got involved with a top NFL quarterback, breaking Risk's heart and hu-miliating him in front of the entire country—the life he'd known all but gone. "Twice Dumped" had been the headline, showing side-by-side photos of him grounded by the stallion and an unflattering pose of him and Shannon.

If only April hadn't seen a recovering Risk guest hosting the Houston rodeo that day. If only she hadn't bumped into him later at the hotel bar. If only he hadn't been so vulnerable and open and kind to her that night, good sense might have prevailed. But they'd really con-nected that night, and his lovemaking led her to think impossible things.

But never in her wildest expectations had she thought he'd walk out on her the next morning without so much as an explanation, a note, a goodbye. It cheap-ened what might have been the best night of her life.

"Okay, I get it."

Risk exhaled, seeming relieved. "You accept my apology?"

If he'd come exclusively to apologize, it surely would've meant more. "Risk, why don't we just drop it and keep our personal lives out of this. Have a seat and we'll get down to the real reason you're here." She couldn't help the jab; he deserved it, and judging by the frown on his face, it hit the mark.

"Fine."

They both sat down, and she pulled the file for the listing. She had one month left on her contract with the owner, Mr. Hall, and selling the $5.3 million lodge would put her struggling agency in the black well into next year.

"Let's focus on the potential of the property," she said.

He nodded, and his gaze roamed over the office, leisurely taking it all in. "But first let me say I like what you've done here. The place never looked this good when it was ole Perry Bueller's shop."

"Mr. Bueller was selling antiques. I had to modernize a bit, but I was hoping to keep some of the charm of the old place."

April had opened her own real estate agency in Boone Springs one year ago with goals to be the premiere high-end listing company in the county. She'd worked for three years in adjacent Willow County learning the ropes and getting her feet wet, but when Perry Bueller decided to retire and sell this storefront property in the heart of Boone Springs, April knew it was time to take action to realize her dream of living and working in her hometown. She'd scraped together the money and transformed his rustic antique store into a modern-day office.

A teardrop crystal chandelier hung from the center of the ceiling, beautiful mahogany bookcases hugged the walls and the computer-topped desks made of the finest polished cherrywood were all pieces generously gifted to her by Mr. Bueller, her late grandmother Beth's dear friend.

"You've done well for yourself, April."

She didn't take Risk's compliment lightly. April had worked hard, and it was nice to be recognized, but she had to keep it in perspective. She couldn't allow herself the luxury of liking Risk again, despite his long overdue apology or his Texas charm.

The last deal she'd worked on had fallen through at the last minute. Six weeks of putting a deal together, all for naught. Her small agency couldn't take another hit like that, and she couldn't pass up the opportunity to sell the unoccupied lodge to the Boones. She had a mortgage to pay, a reputation to build and a desire so deep to make her dream a success, she wasn't about to let her feelings about Risk interfere with her goals. "T-thank you."

She gave Risk the file on Canyon Lake Lodge and pointed to the photos. "As you can see, it's a great piece of property."

"It's remote."

"I like to think of it as secluded, a perfect place for a getaway. The lodge is set back in the hills, miles away from traffic and the town. There's something for everyone, whether it's kicking back and relaxing or outdoor activities. The lake is amazing, and there could be horseback riding and fishing and boating. It's a perfect place for vacationers to experience nature."

"It gives *rustic* a whole new meaning. It's overgrown. Looks like it's falling apart."

She held her breath. "Looks can be deceiving."

"Or they can be dead-on."

"There's wiggle room for negotiation. And there's an intriguing story behind the lodge's history. I have the articles here." She reached into her drawer and came up with a manila folder with articles written about the lodge from sixty years prior. "You can read up on it. The research is fascinating. I have no doubt the lodge could be marketed in a very appealing way when the time comes to book guests."

She set the folder on the desk, and Risk flipped through the articles. "You've done your homework, haven't you?"

"I always do."

Risk looked up from the file just as she did, and their eyes met. A sizzle worked its way down to her toes. She was close enough to breathe in his scent, to be reminded of her fantasy night with him.

"I'm impressed," he drawled in that special way he had.

She jerked back and fiddled with the papers on her desk.

"Mind if I take a better look at these articles?"

"No, of course not. Take them with you."

He rose, and she came around the desk to walk him to the door. When she was standing beside him, he filled her space, and she swallowed hard. "I'd better get back to work. If you have any further questions or would like to see the property, don't hesitate to call. The number is inside the folder."

"Give me a day or two. I'll definitely be in touch."

"Okay, sure."

"Oh, and April?"

She gazed into eyes that had softened on her. He seemed ready to say something but then shook his head. "Never mind."

She closed the door behind him and slumped in relief.

After two years, she'd finally spoken to Risk Boone again.

And because of a possible sale to Boone Inc., she had to hold back on the choice words she'd reserved just for him to hear.

Normally April didn't go out on a work night, but tonight was special. Tonight was her best friend's birthday, and she couldn't let the party go on without her. Jenna Mae turned the big three-oh today; it was monumental. So April donned her black party dress with silver rhinestone straps and met her friends for drinks at the Farmhouse Bar and Grill, a honky-tonk that was always bustling no matter the day of the week.

It was live band Thursday, and Jenna Mae kept glancing at the guitarist up on the platform stage. She was newly single after a disheartening breakup with a guy who didn't know the ass end of a donkey. Jenna was better off without him, and April and Clovie had let her know it. Because that's what friends did. When a storm was brewing, they got out their rain jackets and umbrellas and shielded each other as best they could.

April finished off her first mango margarita as all eight girls swarmed around Jenna Mae at their table near the long, handcrafted Farmhouse bar. They were already an hour into the celebration; gifts had been opened and funny birthday cards passed around.

"Yum, this is delicious," Jenna said, taking a big bite of her cupcake catered by Katie's Kupcakes. "Thanks for this, April. I'm glad you're here. Wouldn't be the same without you."

"I wouldn't have missed it, Jenna. You know that."

Jenna put her arm around April's shoulders. "I do know that. I'm just glad you moved back from Willow County when you did."

"Me, too."

"Are things getting any easier?" Jenna asked. "Sold any big-ass mansions lately?"

"I wish. Actually, I'm waiting to hear back on a potential huge deal. If I land it, it would keep the agency afloat into next year."

The waitress came by with another round of drinks. April wasn't a big drinker, but number two looked good, so she grabbed it up and took a sip.

"I hope it works out for you."

"I'm beginning to have my doubts," she mumbled. "My buyer was supposed to get back to me last week. And I haven't heard a word."

"Why not call and give him a nudge?"

"You won't believe who it is."

Jenna Mae grabbed her arm and pulled her away from the crowd. "Tell me." Jenna was on her third drink, which might just be her limit. She wobbled a little when she walked.

April spoke in Jenna's ear. "It's Risk Boone. If you can believe that."

Jenna knew all about her high school crush and fantasy night with Risk, and so it wasn't surprising that her mouth dropped open. *"No."*

"Yes. He was at the office last week. It was…awkward."

"I can imagine. Man, you crushed on him heavily in high school. You've always had a soft spot for that guy."

"Not anymore. Not after…Houston."

"Really? Because I didn't want to say anything, but he's sitting at the bar right now."

April couldn't believe it; now *her* mouth dropped open. And her heart sped up. She had her back to the bar, and she casually turned to look over her shoulder. Yep, there was Risk, sitting on a stool, flanked by two women, one on each side of him. They were leaning against the bar top, engaging him in conversation. Typical. Women swarmed around Risk like bees to honey. He'd been a big celebrity at one time. It was crazy to think she'd been one of his hangers-on a couple of years ago.

"Oh wow, I've never seen him in here before," Jenna said.

"No, neither have I," she muttered. "When we spoke, he made it seem like he hasn't been in Boone Springs much lately." And April wasn't a regular customer at the Farmhouse. She'd been too busy to go out during the week, and there was a diner closer to her office that delivered.

April was about to look away, a queasy feeling in the pit of her stomach, only to discover that Risk didn't seem to be listening to the women speaking in his ear. His eyes were on her through the reflection in the wide rectangular mirror behind the bar. She was caught in his gaze, her heart pumping hard. There was a moment of awareness, pure and instinctual, that sparked in her veins.

His lips twitched upward. Was he smiling at her?

Oh boy. She stared another half a second then grabbed Jenna's arm. "Let's get back to the table."

A few minutes later, April polished off the rest of her drink as she chatted with her friends who were still seated and not cutting loose on the dance floor. Her head was a little fuzzy, she had a definite buzz going on, and the more she thought about Risk Boone not giving her the courtesy of a return call this week, the more it bugged her.

"I left him two voice mails about the lodge, and he never got back to me," she told Clovie and Jenna. And now he was sitting at the bar smugly, watching her every move. How was she supposed to take that? "I'm gonna talk to him now, whether he likes it or not," she said. As she began to rise, two hands came down on her shoulders, pushing her back down, Clovie from the right and Jenna from the left.

"Wait," Clovie said. "I know that look in your eyes, April. You need to calm down. There's still hope for the deal. You can simply, tactfully ask him what the delay is."

"Clovie's right," Jenna said. "You're a professional. Don't blow it because you're ticked off."

April sighed and nodded, thinking it through. Risk was a rich, handsome hunk, but he'd also been a jerk to her. Still she couldn't let her personal feelings about Risk deter her from her job. "Okay, you guys are right. I'll do that."

"And another thing you're going to do is put this

on." Jenna slid a diamond cluster ring off her right hand. "From now on, you're engaged."

"I'm what?"

"You heard me, you're engaged to be married. It's just a form of insurance when dealing with Risk."

"I can't do that. That's your grandmother's ring."

"It's for a good cause. I know you'll take care with it."

"For heaven's sake, Jenna. I can certainly speak with the man—"

"Whoops, looks like he's heading this way." Jenna pushed the ring onto April's left ring finger. "Remember, you're a professional. *And you're engaged,*" she mouthed softly.

April's head swam, and the next thing she knew, she was standing up facing Risk wearing a ring on her left hand and all the other girls had vanished onto the dance floor.

"Evenin'," he said, the one word pronounced with enough charm to swallow her up. Suddenly, the ring on her finger didn't seem too over-the-top. There was something about Risk that was too darn attractive. Wearing this ring just might be a blessing in disguise. "Do you have a minute to talk?" he asked.

"I, uh, sure. Here?"

Music blasted from the live band, the drummer's rolling solo doing a number on her ears.

He shook his head. "It's too loud in here. Take a walk with me outside?"

She needed to hear what he had to say, and actually

having some privacy would be better to discuss business. "I, uh, sure."

Risk led the way through the packed crowd and she followed behind him, bumping shoulders and ping-ponging through the patrons. A strong hand came out to take hers, and suddenly the bumping stopped, Risk forming a human barrier for her as he led her toward the door. As soon as she stepped foot outside, she shivered.

"Damn, it's cold out here," he said.

She couldn't disagree. She'd left her coat inside the Farmhouse, and not even the dizzying buzz from her second margarita warded off the winter chill.

"Let's go sit in my car—it'll be a lot warmer for you."

"Is it too cold to talk out here?" Her teeth clattered as she said the words.

"In the parking lot?" He smiled. "You tell me."

A blast of wind ruffled her curls, lifting them high in the air and chilling her to the bone. Goodness, she was being silly not wanting to be alone with Risk. She needed to make this deal, and not even having an unorthodox meeting in a client's car should deter her.

"C'mon, my car's over here." Risk took her arm, drawing her close to his body, and the heat radiating off him kept her a bit warmer as they walked to his SUV. He opened the door for her, and she climbed into the passenger seat. "Put this over you," he said, giving her the sheepskin jacket lying on his seat.

It did the trick immediately. The jacket was snug

and warm around her shoulders and arms and was so long it partly covered her legs, too. "Thanks."

He closed the door and wound around to climb into the driver's seat.

And April found herself bundled up, sitting very close to Risk Boone, his male scent drifting her way, his presence filling the space inside the SUV.

"You look real pretty tonight, April." Risk blurted out the first thing he'd noticed about her tonight as he turned to face her.

Her chin went up. "Thank you."

"I didn't expect to see you tonight."

"No, I didn't expect to see you, either. But you promised me a call that I never received. What happened? I guess I wasn't on your radar?"

Quite the contrary. After seeing April last week, he'd thought about her plenty.

He hadn't known her all that well in high school, but when he'd seen her that day in the rodeo stands in Houston, after his life had hit an all-time low, she'd been one friendly face, one person from home he could relate to, and finding her at the hotel bar later that night had been pure luck on his part. They'd sat and talked for hours, and then things had heated up really fast in his hotel room.

"Believe me, you've *been* on my radar."

Her head snapped up at that. Questions filled her eyes, and he wasn't going to answer any of them. "I'm sorry about not returning your voice mails, but I haven't had time to look at the articles about the lodge.

The truth is, I was called out of town. A friend's mother was gravely ill, and she wanted to see me. I felt compelled to go. She was a wonderful, gentle woman that I really cared about."

"Cared? Did she pass on?"

He nodded. "Yes, I stayed in Atlanta for the funeral."

Sympathy touched April's eyes. "I'm sorry."

He kept it to himself that it had been Shannon Wilkes's mother who'd passed on. Shannon had been texting him for months, about her personal life being a hot mess, her career taking a bit of a hit and then her mother's illness. Risk had resolved things with Shannon a while back. Though the scars were still there, he'd realized she wasn't the right woman for him, yet he'd sympathized with Shannon over losing her mother. For the two years he'd dated Shannon, Mary had been like a mother to him, and they'd always gotten along. "Yeah, it was rough."

April gave him a sympathetic nod.

After he ran scared that night in Houston, he wouldn't have blamed April if she refused to work with him. The sale of the lodge was important to her, and he owed her a fair shake, at the very least. "Do you have plans day after tomorrow?" he asked her.

She looked at him skeptically. "Why?"

"Maybe we can drive out to the lodge and take a look at it. I'll read the articles about the place tomorrow. Then I can see for myself if it's doable."

April's eyes brightened. "Yes, I'd love for you to see the lodge. I'll plan on it."

"Okay, good. I've kept you from your friends long enough. Let me walk you back inside."

"No, that's not necessary." She handed him back his coat. "Thanks anyway, but it's a short walk. See you Saturday."

She got out of his car, and he got out, too, and watched, his instincts telling him not to let her walk through the darkened parking lot by herself. And sure enough, when April was less than twenty feet away, a drunken cowboy approached her, blocking her passage, giving her grief and making crude suggestions. Her voice rose as she told the guy to back off, and then the cowboy began grabbing at her. Risk moved fast and was there in seconds, shoving the man's shoulders, pushing him out of the way before he could lay a hand on April. "Buddy, get the hell outta here or you're gonna be real sorry. Go sober up somewhere. Now."

The man eyed Risk with contempt. Risk would be all too happy to nail the guy to the wall, but after a three-second staring contest, the cowboy stalked off.

Risk turned to April. She was shivering, this time in fear. He saw it in her eyes, too. "Are you okay?"

"I…will…be."

He wrapped his arms loosely around her shoulders, bringing her into his warmth. "Come here a sec and calm down."

"Thank…you." She leaned against him, setting her head on his chest as if that's exactly what she'd needed. "That was scary."

"You handled yourself well." He'd heard the tone of her voice, the gruff way she tried to warn the guy off. "You know, the Southern in me would never let a woman walk through a parking lot without seeing her safely inside, but then again, the female revolution has changed all that. I never know what to do."

April pulled away from his chest to gaze up at him, the pretty blue of her eyes damn near mesmerizing. "You did good."

He smiled, and she smiled, too, and something clicked in that moment, a spark that he hadn't felt in a long time. He hadn't met a woman who interested him in months, and now, suddenly, he was thinking about April that way. "I did?"

She gazed at his mouth and nodded. Was it an invitation? In that one second, Risk's body twitched, and he tightened his hold on April. "You did," she whispered.

He laid his palm on her cheek and felt her softness, witnessed the sweet look she was giving him. "April," he said, right before leaning in to brush a soft kiss to her lips.

She moaned a little bit and gave in to the pleasure of his mouth. She tasted sweet and tangy, like a fruity drink, and he started remembering things about her that quickened his pulse.

Then out of the blue, April pulled away quickly, giving him a slight push on the chest. He backed off instantly. What in the world?

"Don't."

"*Don't?* April, did I read you wrong?"

"I've had too much to drink tonight and I do appreciate you protecting me from that drunk, but yes, you read me wrong."

She lifted up her left hand and wiggled her fingers right in front of his nose. "I'm engaged to be married, Risk."

Two

Normally Risk was good at reading women's signals but the other night at the Farmhouse, April had had him fooled. He could've sworn she wanted his attention. She'd looked at him, then at his mouth, as if she'd wanted to be kissed. Had it just been fear? Had she been grateful he'd come on the scene in the parking lot when he had?

April was a beautiful woman with sass and spunk.

And she was engaged to be married.

He'd remembered the chubby little girl she'd been, and when he'd met her again in Houston after he'd guest hosted the rodeo, her curvy body and pretty blue eyes had drawn him in.

"Risk, you're deep in thought this morning." Aunt Lottie poured him a cup of coffee and set the mug down on the kitchen table in front of him. Ever since his aunt had returned to Rising Springs Ranch, she'd doted on him and his two brothers, Mason and Lucas. Having an adventurous spirit, Aunt Lottie had been a world traveler always ping-ponging in and out of their lives, but after the death of their parents, she'd taken a more vital role with the family. And now was like a mother to him and his brothers.

Risk brought the mug to his mouth and sipped. "No one would ever call me a deep thinker."

Lottie took the chair adjacent to him, bringing her coffee to her lips and shaking her head. "You're a fine thinker, boy." Aunt Lottie was the first to come to a Boone's defense, unless of course they deserved a tongue-lashing, and then she'd be the first one to give it. "But something's bothering you. Your aunt knows you boys all too well."

"Nothing's bothering me, really. I'm just baffled about something."

About April. He'd been drawn to her the other night, the same way he'd been drawn to her in Houston. And that was precisely why he hadn't looked her up again. Why he hadn't pursued her after that night. It had been selfish of him, but he hadn't been in any shape to deal with a woman who wasn't a one-night-stand kind of girl. She'd been smart and sincere and compassionate. Once he figured that out, he'd run like hell. Not his finest moment.

"Care to tell me her name?" Aunt Lottie asked.

"Ha, nice try, Aunt Lottie. But it's all good." He winked and gave her his best smile.

"How's Drew doing these days?" he asked.

His aunt had an on-again, off-again relationship with Mason's future father-in-law, Drew MacDonald. It seemed the two of them never could get on the same page.

"I wouldn't know. He's barely talking to me."

"Oh yeah? Lovers' spat?"

Drew lived in the cottage on the Boone property. He was a recovering alcoholic, a good man who'd lost his wife some years ago. Maria had been Lottie's best friend, and now the two were playing a cat and mouse game of hearts.

"Hardly. We're barely friends anymore, Risk."

"Well, why don't you take some of those warm cranberry muffins you just baked and bring them to him as a peace offering?"

Aunt Lottie's blond brows lifted, and her eyes sparkled. She was a pretty sixtysomething woman who had a lot of love to give, and right now she was considering his suggestion. "You know, that's not a bad idea. And while I'm at it, I'll pack you a basket of muffins and some things for your trip."

"Thanks. It's a long drive out to Canyon Lake Lodge."

"Just give me a moment," his aunt said.

Minutes later, after finishing up his breakfast, he heard the front doorbell chime and the housekeeper answer it. He rose, taking the basket Aunt Lottie had made up, and walked out of the kitchen to the parlor where April Adams was waiting for him holding a brown briefcase. Those curly blond locks of hers flowed past her shoulders, and even the tan winter coat she wore over a pair of pants and a sweater couldn't hide her curvy body.

"Mornin', April. You're right on time," he said, coming into the room.

"I always try to be." She hoisted her chin up.

"I'll be right with you," he said.

He grabbed his sheepskin jacket, the one he'd lent April the other night, and showed her to the multicar garage attached to the house.

In the garage, he opened the passenger side door to his full-size SUV. He'd insisted he drive his car, and she was clearly not happy about it. April shot him a look and then climbed in. He waited while she buckled herself in and then handed her the basket.

"What's this?"

"My aunt Lottie made us a care package for the road."

"That's…very sweet of her."

"The Boones *are* nice people," he said.

Her eyes started to roll, and then she seemed to catch herself. Risk almost laughed out loud when her expression changed to an innocent smile. The trouble was he liked April Adams. Too damn much.

Risk started the engine and pulled out of the garage. There were gray skies overhead, and a light drizzle cascaded down from the clouds.

With any luck, they'd drive right out of the rain to better weather up ahead.

The rain came down steadily now, giving the windshield wipers a good workout. Of course, the weather

had to be gloomy; it would make it that much harder for
April to show off the grounds in a good light to Risk.
But she didn't want to turn back. She couldn't trust
that she'd get Risk back out to Canyon Lake Lodge any
time soon.

She stared out the window, trying to think of ways
to enhance her sales pitch. The lodge had been listed
with her agency for five months, and she only had the
listing for one more month. That gave her only weeks
to find a buyer. The Boones' inquiry about the property had been the only real bite she'd gotten in all that
time. She had to make this work, somehow. Risk hadn't
been overly impressed with the photos of the lodge,
and that parking lot kiss had only put a strain on their
professional relationship.

"Cold?" he asked.

"A little."

He fiddled with a dashboard dial, and soon a flow
of warm heat pushed out of the floor vents.

"Better?"

She nodded. "Yes, thank you. As long as it's not
too hot for you?"

He gave her a sideways glance. "I'll let you know
if it gets too hot."

Was that an innocent comment? She never knew
with Risk. But she had to give him the benefit of the
doubt, since he'd been put in his place the other night
after she'd told him she was engaged.

Thank you again, Jenna Mae.

They drove a few more miles in silence, and then

Risk gestured to the basket. "Since Aunt Lottie packed us up some food, why don't we have a muffin?"

"Sounds like a good idea." She lifted the basket onto her lap and then folded back the lid. "Oh wow. Your aunt Lottie sure knows how to make a care package."

"Why, what's she got in there?"

"Well, let's see. There's about eight muffins, a coffee thermos, protein bars and two apples."

A grumble rose from Risk's throat. "She still thinks we're twelve."

"It's sorta sweet that she cares so much."

April picked up a muffin, peeled back the cupcake paper, removing it entirely, and handed it over to Risk. It seemed an intimate gesture, but it was easier for him to eat that way. "Here you go."

"Thanks." A few bites later, the muffin was gone. "Want another?"

He nodded. "One more will do. Make sure you have one, too."

"Oh, I intend to." April took a bite of her muffin. Warm and fresh, packed with cranberries, it was just the right amount of sweet and tart. "These are good."

"It's a family recipe. That coffee smells good."

"Want some?"

The wipers were at top speed now, and April hoped Risk wouldn't suggest they turn back.

"You first," he said. "Have some. It'll warm you up inside."

"Okay. Thanks."

She unscrewed the thermos and poured coffee into the cup. As she took a sip, the pungent aroma comforted her and made her smile. She handed the thermos over to Risk, and their fingers brushed again. "H-here you go." The contact wasn't lost on her. She quelled her racing heart and watched his throat work as he gulped down coffee.

Risk slid a glance to her left hand. "When's the wedding?"

Whoa. She wasn't really prepared to answer him. She'd hoped that wearing the ring was enough. Apparently she was wrong. "Uh, we haven't set the date yet."

"No?"

"No. A…a lot goes into planning a wedding, and my fiancé and I are very busy."

"Does he have a name?"

"Everyone has a name," she said rather evasively.

Risk scratched his chin. "So, you're not willing to tell me? He must not be—"

"He's amazing, okay? I met him when I was living in Willow County, and we're very happy."

"Bob? Bill? Toby? Or maybe it's more like Hector or Bubba?"

Bubba? Lordy. She folded her arms over her middle but still couldn't hold back a belly chuckle. "Risk, what are you doing?"

"Just making conversation. It's a long drive to the lodge. Especially with the rain slowing us down."

"Okay then, if you're so willing to talk, why don't you tell me about your love life?"

He grunted. "Or lack thereof."

She raised her brows. "That's hard to believe."

"Tell me about it. After what happened with Shannon, I think I got gun-shy. No more permanent, all-in relationships for me."

"Are you saying you don't date anymore?"

He spared her a glance, his dark eyes meeting hers. "Now who's being nosy?"

"Okay, you're right. Forget I asked." It wasn't fair of her to ask such pointed questions of Risk when she'd barely given him the time of day about her fake engagement.

He was silent for a while. "The truth is, I haven't had a date in three months, maybe longer. I guess I lost count."

"I see. So, you must be really into your work, the way I am."

Risk's mouth twisted, and he gave his head a small, almost inconspicuous shake. "I'm trying to help out. The truth is…"

"What?" She gave him a pointed look.

"Nothin'."

She let it drop, because anybody with eyes in their head could tell that Risk wasn't the tycoon his brothers were. If he was, he wouldn't have become a rodeo rider.

"What did you think about the history of the lodge?" she asked, steering the conversation out of personal territory.

"Kinda crazy…neither one of them wanted to give in for the sake of success."

"So, you did read the articles."

"I surely did. That brother and sister team mixed as well as oil and water."

April nodded. "I don't have a brother or a sister, but

I would think one of them could've given in rather than see the lodge fail."

"Yeah, those two were doomed from the get-go."

It was sort of like her and Risk. Doomed from the beginning.

Luckily, because of the ring on her finger, all she had to think about was convincing Risk that the lodge was worth the investment.

Halfway into the drive, Risk turned to April. "The storm's not really letting up. Let me know if you want to turn back."

"No," April said firmly. "I don't think we need to. We've come this far."

"Okay, fine by me." Risk didn't want to turn around, either. He wasn't opposed to driving in the rain, and he was sort of enjoying the adventure with her. He'd been in a rut lately, trying to figure out where he fit in the world.

He liked listening to April's melodic voice as she went into detail about JoAnna and Joseph Sutton, the twins who'd inherited the lodge some sixty years ago from their great-aunt. Her take on it was certainly more passionate and animated than any conversation they'd had before.

"JoAnna was a woman of the earth," she said, "a free spirit who wanted to use the lodge as refuge for the enlightened of heart. She wanted bonfire parties and folksy dances, while Joseph was a hard-core outdoorsman who wanted to keep the rustic tone and promote it as a boating and fishing lodge."

"Must've made for some crazy interaction between the guests," he said. "Can you imagine the hunters and fisherman going head to head with the vegetarians? I'm sure it wasn't pretty."

"It was a total failure. Finally, they sold the lodge to a recluse. He liked the fact that it was remote, off the beaten path."

"Is he the one selling the lodge?"

"No, he passed on. We'd be dealing with his grandson, Michael Hall. I can't wait to show it to you. If we ever make it there."

"We will, trust me," Risk said, just as he hit a pothole in the road. The SUV bounded up in the air and landed with a huge muddy splash.

April gripped the handrail, color draining from her face.

"You okay?"

She gave him an unsure nod.

He reached for her hand clutching the seat and gave it a slight squeeze. "We'll be fine. The SUV can take it."

She slid her hand from his and slunk back in her seat, warily folding her arms across her middle.

There wasn't much else he could say, so he shut his trap. It was better to forget the solid connection he'd felt when he grabbed her hand a few seconds ago. She was pretty and intelligent, and touching her quickened his pulse. For a man who hadn't had sex in a while, it was dangerous territory.

And he wasn't forgetting about that engagement ring on her finger. No, sir.

Rain pelted the windshield, and he concentrated on driving through the storm, the wipers giving him glimpses of what was ahead. He came to a low-lying bridge just around a curve in the road and slowed the car as the long wooden planks rattled under the tires. "It won't be long now," he told April and took a right-hand turn down a tree-lined road. April's face relaxed in relief.

A minute later, the road separated into a three-foot-wide ditch. "Holy crap." He swerved instantly, missing the biggest part of the gouge in the road, but luck wasn't with him. The car hit the very edge of the gap, and the front end plummeted into a gully of mud. He hinged his arm out to stop April's momentum, while her seat belt did the rest.

"You okay?" he asked her.

"Yeah, I think so." Color left her face. "W-what happened?"

"The rain washed away a good chunk of the road. It came up so fast, I couldn't see it, but I think we're on the edge of the ditch."

"Are we stuck?"

"Afraid so. The good news is GPS says the lodge is less than a mile away."

She sat silent for a few seconds. "And you can't get us out of the ditch?"

"Unfortunately, I left my superhero cape back at the ranch. We can't just sit here. We might sink farther into the ditch. Gather up your things, April."

He needed to make sure she was safe, and that meant high-tailing it to the lodge before the storm worsened. "We need to make a run for it. I'll get out first and help you. We'll call for help when we're safely at the lodge."

He gathered up a few essentials from the back of the SUV and dumped them into an old duffel bag he kept in the back. When he opened his door slightly, a wild gust of wind blew it open the rest of the way. He jumped down into a foot of mud, his boots catching the brunt of the ooze. Tossing the bag over his shoulder, he made his way around the back end of the SUV and opened the door for April. "Got what you need?"

She tucked her briefcase and her purse under her coat and nodded.

Risk reached for her, his hands firmly on her waist, and lifted her out of the car, holding on tight and twirling her around until they were clear of the ditch entirely before he set her down. "Ready to go?"

"I'm ready."

"Okay, let's get out of here." He took her hand and they trudged along the waterlogged road toward the lodge.

April had never been this soaked in her life. The mile sprint had her breathing heavily, but she was in good enough shape to keep up with Risk, who kept a tight grip on her hand. They hopped over potholes and dodged floating debris and then, finally, the sight of the lodge loomed like a big beautiful refuge. She hadn't been happier to see anything in her life.

Minutes later, they took the wide river-rock stairs together and landed under the protection of a covered veranda. Rain ceased to pelt them now, and the low veranda walls broke the wind gusts.

Risk stood by the double-door entry. "You have the key?"

Shaking from the cold, she opened the briefcase she'd kept as dry as possible and handed Risk the key. "H-here you go."

He opened the door and gestured for her to go inside. She'd been here twice before and remembered the layout. Risk followed directly behind her, a consoling presence after the ordeal they'd just been through. For a moment there, when the earth parted and the car careened into the ditch, she'd feared for her life. But Risk was there beside her, making her feel safe. Right now, it went a long way in reassuring her.

"Stay here while I check out the place and see if the power's on."

"It's supposed to be. Mr. Hall is keeping the electricity on through the sale."

Risk nodded and took off while she stood there, shivering. She scanned the interior of the main lobby. It had a floor-to-ceiling river-rock fireplace and settees positioned around the large room. Thick wood beams crisscrossed the tall ceilings, and black iron chandeliers hung from various points in the room. Though the room was cold, it was shelter from the raging storm outside.

"Looks like the storm knocked the power out," Risk said upon his return. "But there's some firewood here on the hearth, and I'm sure it's enough to keep us warm until the storm clears."

A puddle of water formed at her feet, droplets dripping from her clothes, her coat, her hair.

"I think that's a good idea."

"Give me a second to get a fire going."

While he was building a fire, she removed her coat and foraged inside her drenched handbag for her cell phone. Checking the screen, she wasn't surprised she had no service. Even on a good weather day, the cell service out here had been spotty. Now, it seemed nonexistent. She imagined the same was true of Risk's cell.

She walked over to the massive fireplace, where Risk was stacking logs. She found a magazine lying on one of the tables and rolled it up. "You can use this for kindling."

"That'll work."

She slapped it into his palm and shivered again. "I don't suppose you checked your phone yet."

"The minute we got inside. No service. You?" He tossed the kindling under the logs and lit it up.

"Same. Nothing."

Just then the kindling caught, and a small fire crackled and flamed. The burst of color also lent warmth, and she scooted closer to the new blaze.

Risk turned to her. "We should get out of our wet clothes. Get dry."

She blinked. She couldn't believe he'd suggested it. "How do you suppose we do that?"

"Peel 'em off."

"That's not what I meant. I don't have a change of clothes."

"Neither do I. But there's got to be towels or bed-

ding or something we can wrap ourselves up in until
our clothes dry out." He gave her an up and down
glance. "Unless you want to shiver yourself into pneu-
monia."

Uh, no. She didn't want to do that, but she couldn't
bring herself to say it. Risk caught her dumbfounded
look and shook his head.

"April, you've got nothing to worry about with me.
That ring on your finger might as well be a chastity
belt. I'm only suggesting we don't catch our death of
cold in these wet clothes. Should only take an hour or
so to dry them."

She stared at the blaze burning bright orange, the
glow rapidly growing. Risk was right, and boy, she
hated to admit it, but the fire would dry out their clothes
in no time. And that comment he made about her engagement ring hit home. She believed he'd be true to
his word. "Okay. Let's see if we can find something to
wrap up in. There's a master bedroom and a few other
rooms on the ground level. I think Mr. Hall said he
stays over once in a while."

"Sounds good to me." Risk walked over to where
he'd dropped his duffel and came up with a utility
lantern flashlight. He pulled the handle, and the light
came on, flashing a halo over six feet of the room.
"We'll use this only if we need to. Want to save the
charge for tonight."

"Tonight?"

Risk turned to look her square in the eye. "The
storm's going strong, and we're stuck. It's doubtful
we'll get out of here today."

Thunder boomed, making her jump. She hadn't really thought that far ahead. "Won't someone come looking for us?"

Risk shrugged. "Don't know. Most around here must think this place is empty. No one's lived here for years, right?"

She nodded.

"And with the rain coming down in buckets and the car sunk in the mud…"

"Oh." A few seconds ticked by. "What about your family? Will they come looking?"

Risk smiled, his deadly dimples making an appearance. "My brothers know I'm smart enough to get out of the way of the storm. Wouldn't be the first time I didn't make it home at night."

April bit her lower lip. "I see. And your aunt?"

"Goes to bed kinda early. She probably figured I'd get in late."

That left Clovie. She was the only one April had told about this trip. And she wasn't due in the office until Monday afternoon.

It was her own fault for getting in this predicament. She should've postponed the meeting when the weather turned bad or at least asked Risk to turn back when the storm first hit. Now, she had to spend the night…with him. And soon they were going to get naked.

"Don't worry. We'll make do. We have some food, thanks to Aunt Lottie."

"You brought the basket?"

"Yep." He pointed to his duffel. "Now, let's go find us some warm things. Which way?"

She pointed to the passage to the left and then followed Risk down a murky hallway to a big double door. "This is the private master bedroom."

Risk opened the door, and they peered inside to a bedroom filled with just enough light to see a king-size bed made up with blankets and a quilt. They stepped into the room and began rummaging through a chest of drawers, and it was like finding a trove of precious treasures. They found extra blankets and sheets and candles. The furniture was large and sparse, made of solid wood. A fireplace sat against the far wall, and one big window faced out to angry gray clouds and pounding rain.

Risk grabbed two of the blankets and a big sheet. "This should do for now. You want to get out of your clothes in here? I'll get mine off in the lobby." He handed her the blanket, not really waiting for a reply, and walked out of the room.

She made quick work of peeling off her clothes, shoes first. She'd have to put her modesty on hold out of necessity. Just thinking about putting on dry, warm clothes again, undies included, made her heart sing.

She gathered up her clothes, wound herself up good and tight in the big blanket like a fruity roll up, and made her way to the lobby. Risk, casually wrapped in his blanket, had already set out a sheet for them to sit on between the two settees close to the fire. His clothes were laid out on his half of the hearth. She remembered he was a boxer kind of guy. Images popped into her head of that one night they'd had together. It had been pure magic, but that magic had vanished like a swift bird in flight the very next morning. No matter. She forced her gaze away from his clothes and proceeded to lay out her pants and top on the hearth. It was hard to be discreet with her undies no matter how she tried to conceal them, so she gave up and laid them out at the far end of the hearth. They'd be the first to dry anyway, comprised of far less material than her other clothes.

She took a seat facing the fire, allowing the warmth to seep into her skin. "Ah, this feels so good."

Risk gazed at her soaking up the heat and smiled. "Gotta admit this is a first for me."

"I'm afraid to ask."

"Being naked, enjoying a fire with a beautiful woman and not—"

"Don't say it, Risk." She shook her head. "Don't say it."

"And not having anything to offer but muffins and protein bars."

That was so *not* what he was going to say, but she smiled anyway. "Right now, a protein bar sounds pretty good."

His head snapped up. "Are you hungry?"

"I could eat."

"I'll get the food."

As he rose, the blanket around his shoulders slipped, exposing his granite chest and an incredible amount of sinewy muscles. Firelight glowed over his face and upper body, and she reacted with a sharp breath. It wasn't fair for a guy to look so darn good.

Luckily for her, she'd learned a hard lesson with him, so no amount of good looks could take away from what he'd done to her. He hadn't had the good grace to tell her face-to-face that he wasn't available in any way, and his abandonment had really hurt.

When she was six years old, her father had deserted her and her mother. That's when she'd begun eating heavily. Even though her rational brain knew Risk's actions were all on him, a part of her had reverted to that plump little girl who'd been abandoned by her father, the chubby girl who'd been invisible to most, as if people looked right past her, not really seeing her for the person she was.

But today, Risk was on his best behavior and he'd made her feel safe—as safe as a woman could feel, being naked under this blanket, having a meal with an equally naked-under-the-blanket guy, sitting by a luminous fire.

"Here you go," he said, bringing the food basket with him. "One protein bar coming up." He tossed it to her and as her arm came up to catch the bar, her blanket dipped, exposing her shoulders and, maybe, a teeny tiny bit of her cleavage.

Oh boy.

Risk's brows rose. He hadn't missed a thing.

A deep sigh escaped his lungs as he fell back against the base of the settee and bit into his protein bar. Still chewing, he glanced into the fire. "Maybe you should tell me all about this fiancé of yours."

Three

April's mouth gaped open. Risk's statement rubbed her the wrong way. What about his claims that her engagement ring was like a chastity belt? Was one glimpse at her bare shoulders enough to change his mind? If she wasn't so floored, her ego might have bumped up. "I have a better idea. Why don't you tell me all about Shannon Wilkes."

Risk stopped chewing and turned to her. "Why?"

"You seem so intent on my love life, but what about yours?"

"I don't usually talk about it."

"No kidding."

His mouth twisted at her sardonic tone. "My love life was plastered all over the tabloids. Couldn't pass a

newsstand without seeing Shannon's face on the cover
with her new guy."

"But that's not your story."

"Nobody wants to hear my story."

"I do."

He shook his head and stared into the flames again.
"Why go there?"

"To help me understand what happened that night."

"Look, I blew it with you and I'm sorry. I was in
a bad place."

"So you've said. What happened between you and
Shannon?"

Risk remained silent. He finished his protein bar,
his face turned to the flames rocketing like shooting
stars in the massive fireplace. Safe from the storm outside and huddled in warmth, she could think of nothing she wanted to hear more than Risk's take on his
life. At least she'd done one thing: diverted his attention from her made-up fiancé.

She, too, stared at the mesmerizing flames. It was
peaceful and quiet sitting there together absorbing heat
and trying to relax.

"There's nothing much to tell," Risk said, his voice
low and deep. "She blindsided me, and it wasn't pretty."

Surprised that he'd said anything, April pursed her
lips and listened.

"I met Shannon at a charity banquet to raise funds
for children of military families. My brother Lucas was
a Marine, and this was something near and dear to him.
Shannon used her celebrity to persuade donors to help,
and I was very impressed with her. She knew how to

dazzle, and apparently, she dazzled me, too. I was all in with her, at the height of my game, winning rodeo after rodeo, and we were like some high-powered couple. Shannon seemed to bask in all that. But for me, I liked the challenge of the rodeo, of mastering something and being the best, but I didn't need or want all the added attention of dating an actress. We would argue about it. We'd be out somewhere together, and all of sudden there'd be a swarm of reporters snapping pictures, asking nosy questions. And then I'd find out it was all pre-arranged by Shannon's publicist."

"That wasn't the life you signed up for, was it?" April asked.

"I'm a Boone—a town was named for my family—but I never flaunted that or wanted to rub people's noses in it. And I never made a big deal about it. Believe it or not, I'm a private kind of guy. But we loved each other. We'd been together for two years and I was ready to take the next step."

She mouthed *marriage*.

"Yeah," he acknowledged. "But then my career came to a careening halt when I busted up my shoulder. It killed me that I couldn't do what I loved to do anymore. But what was worse, Shannon pretty much abandoned me. She hardly came to visit me when I was recuperating, and then she broke it off. The next thing I know…she's with Todd Alden, the NFL quarterback, and their pictures were splashed all over the news."

"That's pretty low," April said.

"That's how I found out Shannon was only using me to make her star rise."

"Must have hurt you badly."

His pride had him shrugging it off, but pain flashed in his eyes for a moment. "I'm over her now. Shannon wasn't right for me. Our lives are completely different, and at least we've managed to get past it. But I'll never allow anyone to make a fool out of me. That's not happening again.

"Back in Houston, the last thing I wanted to do that day was host the rodeo. But then I recognized you sitting in the stands and you smiled at me, and I felt ten times better. You reminded me of home, and in that moment, that's exactly what I needed."

"If it wasn't me, it would've been some other girl."

"Not true," he said adamantly. "I didn't expect to share my bed with a woman that night, but you were warm and bubbly and you made me laugh and forget things that were haunting me."

"I was a distraction."

He sighed and looked away, glancing out the rain-soaked window. "Want to know what I really thought?"

He paused, and April's heart began to pound. Was she ready to hear this? "Go on."

"I thought you were sweet and giving, a woman who wasn't starving herself to get a stick-thin body. I loved your curves and your confidence and your compassion. It was refreshing and…"

"And what?"

"Pretty damn hot, April." He glanced at her engagement ring again. "But in the morning, I had regrets. Not about you, but about me. I wasn't ready for any kind of involvement. It wasn't fair to you, I know, but just thinking about getting involved again so soon after I'd been burned wasn't happening. I should've told you that before taking you up to my hotel room. I should've been honest about my feelings. I knew you were the kind of woman who deserved that much from me. So I took off, vowing to call you and make amends."

"You never did."

"No. I should have, but I didn't. I'm sorry about it."

"So am I." She sighed.

"Now you know my deal with Shannon Wilkes. Enough said."

Well, yes. It explained a lot about his relationship with the movie star, but April still couldn't give him a pass on ditching her after a pretty incredible night of sex. Yes, he'd apologized already, but April wasn't ready to let him off the hook. He'd hurt her, and it had taken a long time to recover from that encounter, to get over her feelings of abandonment.

"You should've tried to reach me. To explain. I didn't leave that hotel room feeling very good about myself. You don't even want to know what I thought about you."

Risk had the good grace to squeeze his eyes shut. "Oh man, April, I deserve that. What can I say?"

She shrugged. "It's over and done with." And at least she'd now let her feelings be known. That was something. He wasn't going to let a woman make a fool out of him again? Well, she felt the same way: no man was ever going to play her for a fool and hurt her again, either.

That much she and Risk Boone had in common.

* * *

Thirty minutes later, April said, "I'm thirsty." They'd finished off what was left of the coffee in the thermos after their protein bar lunch. What sounded good to her now was a cold drink of water.

"The plumbing is working," Risk said.

"Amen to that. Our clothes are dry enough. Why don't we get dressed and go exploring? Might as well check the place out since we're stuck here. We'll explore the kitchen first."

"Fine by me. The fire's dying out anyway."

"There's dry wood outside in the woodshed," she commented. "I'll take the bedroom again to get dressed." She scooped up her warmed clothes from the hearth, anxious to get them back on. It was just too weird sitting in front of a fire, alone with Risk, knowing both of them were naked underneath.

Minutes later in her dry clothes, she went in search of Risk and found him fully dressed, checking out the kitchen facilities. The lodge's eatery had three sets of wide double doors that brought sunlight in on good days and kept the dining room cheerful.

"Well, we won't starve," Risk said. She liked the way his wet hair had dried, falling into his eyes. He'd shake his head and shift the pesky tendrils off his face. The move wasn't lost on her and she'd often catch herself staring at him.

"Uh, what?"

Risk raided the pantry. "There's a bag of potato chips and peanut butter in here. And we still have muffins and fruit from the basket."

"I guess that's luck, if we can say anything about this trip is lucky."

Risk turned on the faucet and let the water run for a while. "Just getting the cobwebs out of the pipes," he said. Then he rinsed out his thermos and filled it with water. "Have a drink," he said to her.

Accepting the thermos, she took a long, cool drink of water. When down to the bare essentials, there really wasn't anything better than water to sustain you. She gulped down the rest and handed the thermos back to Risk. He took his turn guzzling water. The thought of them sharing the thermos no longer seemed weird. It was almost as if they were on some sort of survival camping trip.

With Risk looking on, April took a few minutes to open all the cabinets. A couple of them were about ready to fall off their hinges. She opened drawers and found some off their tracks. All surface stuff. The kitchen was outdated, but the foundation was sturdy.

"The kitchen has a lot of potential. It's large and roomy, and that's a plus when cooking for many guests," she said, going into full Realtor mode.

Risk folded his arms across his middle. "But this entire room would have to be gutted. It needs a fresh start, and we're talking a major overhaul."

"But it would be your overhaul. You could do anything you wanted in here. You could go simple or sophisticated."

Risk's eyes narrowed on her. "Do you really like this place, or are you only trying to make a sale?"

"Both. I do love this lodge. I see the possibilities.

And I think it's a good investment for your family's business, Risk. I do. So, do you want to see the rest?" She pointed up toward the second story.

"Sure, it's not like there's too much else to do around here."

Showing the lodge in the midst of a storm was not the best way to entice a potential client. Risk was losing interest with each passing minute. Upstairs they found the roof leaking in three of the rooms and made quick work of finding bowls and vases to catch the water.

Twenty minutes later, they climbed down the staircase in the lobby. Low-lying embers did little to warm the room, and they both shivered. "You said there's a woodshed outside?" Risk asked.

"Yes," April said. "It's around the right side of the house."

"All right, fine. I'll go get us some firewood for tonight."

"Right now?"

"Better now while there's still some daylight than later tonight."

April bit her lip. The storm was fierce. It hadn't let up. "It's really coming down out there."

"It'll be fine. I'll be back in five minutes. While I'm doing that, why don't you fix us some dinner?"

She stared at him and shook her head. "Oh sure, when you get back, I'll have a five-course meal waiting for you."

He smiled. "I'd expect no less."

* * *

Risk put on his sheepskin coat and plopped his hat low on his forehead. He gave April a nod and grabbed the doorknob. Her expression seemed bleak; she was worried about him. "Be careful."

Her hair had dried into big blond curls that cascaded down her back in a style women paid big money for, but on her the curls were natural. He'd enjoyed watching them fall into place by the fire. Her usually bright blue eyes dimmed as she gave him a little wave.

"Always," he said, opening the door. A shot of wind blew into the room, pushing him back. He fought the force and stepped outside, pulling the door shut behind him.

Rain pummeled the ground as he made a run for the shed, his boots kicking up mud. The entire front yard was flooded, and he splashed his way to the right side of the house. He found the woodshed easily, and just like April had said, there was no lock. Gripping one of the double door handles, he pulled back hard, and the door creaked open. He stepped inside, and now protected somewhat from the storm, he glanced around the roomy shed. Roomy only because there was precious little wood left. Two bundles lay by the back wall, and he figured it was better than nothing. It should be enough to keep them warm for the night in the big drafty lodge.

He lifted the first bundle of firewood, piling a good amount in his arms. The wind blew the shed door shut, so he planted his boot against the door and kicked it

open again. He made his way back to the lodge entrance and dropped the wood right by the front door.
Taking a deep breath, he ventured out again to get the
last of the firewood. Branches from the mesquite trees
nearby all swayed to the right from the terrific gales,
and he moved even faster now to get into the shed.

Once there, he bundled the last pile in his arms
and made a run for it. He was nearly to the front of
the lodge when something loud cracked behind him.
He turned just in time to see a thick tree branch break
from a mesquite tree and jettison his way. He ducked,
but he wasn't fast enough.

The branch struck him in the head, and his knees
buckled before everything went black.

April slathered peanut butter on the leftover muffins, set out the bag of potato chips and put two plump
red apples out for dessert on the kitchen table. "There,
how's that for a feast?" she muttered.

She felt at odds with the universe not having cell
service. No weather reports to look up, no way to com-
municate with loved ones. Yet she wouldn't want anyone venturing out in this storm to come save them.
She'd never seen it so bad. Shutters rattled, the wind
blew unmercifully, the ground flooded.

She hated to admit defeat, but Risk hadn't seen
much he liked in this old lodge. He was seeing it as
a bad investment, while in her mind the place only
needed surface repairs and some tender loving care.
Which meant enduring the day and night together was
all for naught. "Guess I'm not making this sale."

She stared out the window for a while, watching the never-ending downpour. Then she rearranged her scant excuse for dinner, trying to make it look like more than it was, before heading off to use the bathroom facilities. By the time she returned to the kitchen, five minutes had long passed. Yet Risk was still out there.

A moan sounded from the lobby entrance, a low groaning that could be the wind, yet her instincts said differently, and she raced to the front door. Bracing herself, she pulled it open.

And there stood Risk. Well, he was barely standing, his shoulders hunched, blood trickling from a gash on his head. "Risk! My God, what happened to you?"

He stared at her, looking totally bewildered, and slumped into her arms. She had just enough strength to catch him. Using her steam and some of his, she walked him inside. He wasn't talking, and she feared he was in shock. At that moment, she made a quick decision to get him into the master bedroom. He needed care, and that room was easier to heat and had a big comfy bed. "Stay with me, Risk. Hang on."

She took it slow, and they made their way through the lobby, down the hall to the master bedroom they'd raided just hours ago. He was drenched, his coat and pants a muddy mess. "Can you stand while I get off your wet clothes?"

He nodded, barely. She didn't have much time. She had to see to the gash on his head, but she couldn't let him sit in soaked clothes. She got his jacket off first, and then his shirt. "Okay, now let's get you down on the bed." He swayed, and she grabbed him the best she could to keep him from falling, then guided him onto the bed. She took his boots off and then worked at the zipper of his jeans and slid them off. He began to shiver, so she covered him quickly with a blanket, tucking him in tight and hoping he hadn't gone into shock.

"I'll be right back," she whispered.

She ran into the master bathroom, grabbed all of the towels and dashed back to Risk. Now he was out cold. With shaky hands she dabbed at the blood, clearing it away so she could see the extent of the injury. The gash didn't look too deep, but then she wasn't a nurse, so she really had no idea how serious this was. But a nice lump was forming underneath it. Something had hit him hard enough to knock him out.

As she continued to dab, he moaned. Then his eyes slowly opened. That had to be a good thing.

"Risk, can you hear me?" she asked in a loud voice.

He nodded, and then his eyes closed again.

Her heart pounded. She hated seeing anyone hurt, much less someone she cared about.

She cared about Risk?

Only in a Good-Samaritan way. He needed help, and she was it.

"Don't worry. You're going to be all right."

The one thing she did know was if he had a concussion, she couldn't let him sleep. She would have to watch over him for the rest of the day and night. She could do that. She had to.

The room was frigid. Even under the blankets, Risk was shivering. She needed to warm him up with a fire. She left him only for a second, recalling in the back of her mind she'd seen wood on the ground near the front door. After dashing there, she found a bundle he must've dropped near the lodge entrance. She hauled the fire logs inside and into the master bedroom along with another magazine she'd snatched up from the lobby for kindling.

"Are you awake?" she called loudly, tossing the logs into the hearth.

His eyes opened again. *Thank goodness.*

She'd never been a Girl Scout, but she managed to get the kindling lit and tease the logs enough to make a low-lying fire come to life.

She went back to Risk to check his wound. It had stopped bleeding, and gratitude filled her heart. He looked so out of it, so vulnerable, so entirely dumbfounded.

"You're not bleeding anymore, but I'm gonna wrap your head with this clean towel, just in case there's seepage. Let me know if it hurts."

She carefully folded the towel into a thin length and wrapped it around his head to cover the wound. "There. How are you feeling, Risk?"

Fire crackled, and a small blast of light shined on his face. "Who are you? And…why are you calling me Risk?"

Four

April stared at him. For one second she thought he was joking. But then good sense seeped in. He was in no shape to joke, not after the blow to his head... Even an Oscar winner couldn't pull off his total sense of bafflement. "W-what do you mean?"

"You...keep...calling me...Risk."

"Yes, that's your name. Risk Boone. Don't you remember?"

He seemed to search his mind, and the blank look on his face really worried her.

"No. I can't remember anything."

"You can't remember *anything*?" she repeated, swallowing hard.

He thought about it a few seconds more, appearing puzzled. "Not about myself, no."

Oh boy, if that were true then this situation just went from bad to worse. Could he really have…amnesia? The sharp knock to his head would've provoked it, but how long would his memory loss last? And what was she supposed to do about it?

"W-what happened to me?"

"You went out in the storm to get firewood. I think a branch broke off a tree and downed you."

He took that in, not seeming to recall it at all.

"What kind of name is Risk anyway?" he muttered.

Maybe if she talked to him about his life, it would stir a memory or two. "It's not really your name. Your real name is River Boone. And most people who don't know you very well think you got your name because you took a lot of risks on the rodeo circuit. It was sort of your brand. But the truth is your little brother, Lucas, couldn't say River very well when he was a baby. It always came out like *Risker*. The name stuck, and soon everyone was calling you Risk."

She'd learned that bit of trivia when she'd spent the night with him in Houston.

"Oh." None of what she'd said seemed to register with him and he frowned. "What's your name?"

"I'm… I'm April Adams."

"Should I know you?"

"Well…yes. But don't worry about that right now. Let me tell you about your family and maybe you'll recall something."

"You said I had a brother?"

"Yes, two brothers, actually. Mason and Lucas. You all live on Rising Springs Ranch in Boone Springs."

He shook his head slightly, obviously not recognizing the names.

"Your family founded the town a hundred years ago."

He closed his eyes. "I don't..."

"It'll come to you in time," she assured him, hoping that was truly the case.

"Tell me more." Even in his weakened state, he seemed desperate to find something he could relate to, something that might spur a memory.

"You were in the rodeo. Actually, you did really well as a bronc buster. But you hurt your shoulder after a toss from a horse named Justice and needed surgery," she said quietly. She ran her finger along the outline of the injury on his shoulder. "The scar is right here."

He peered deep into her eyes, searching for something. Touching him like that was a mistake, one she couldn't afford to make. Seeing him feeling weak, vulnerable and puzzled jostled something deep in her soft mushy heart.

"I, uh, I'll go get you some water. You need to drink."

She didn't know that for a fact, but the body always needed water. Then images of the storm popped into her head. Outside there was an obscene amount of water flooding the property.

"Don't go," he pleaded. The desperation in his voice made her freeze in place. "Stay here."

There was pain on his face and fear in his eyes. He didn't want to be alone, and she couldn't blame him. He didn't know who he was. He didn't know what had happened to him. To have your mind cleared of all your personal memories had to be unbelievably difficult. "I, uh, okay," she said. "I'll stay."

April watched over him, telling him about how bad the storm was and how they'd made a run for it to the lodge for safety. But he was drifting in and out despite how hard she tried to keep him engaged. As the fire burned low, the room got increasingly colder, and she finally relented and climbed under the covers to keep warm.

He turned toward her.

"It's important you stay awake a little while longer," she whispered, touching her fingers to his cheek. "Please, Risk."

He caught the glimmer of her diamond ring in the last of the firelight and grabbed her hand. Forcing his attention there, his voice lightened and a warm glow entered his eyes. It was the most life she'd seen out of him since she'd found him outside the lodge. "April, we're engaged?"

She was in bed with him, tending to his wounds. Anyone might assume that, but as she opened her mouth to deny it, his lips pressed into the palm of her hand, and the sweetness of the warm kiss he placed there crushed her denial. She should have pulled her hand away and climbed out of the bed, but the brightness on his face, the relief in his eyes, stopped her. It was as if he'd discovered something about himself, his connection to her, and it was hard to destroy his hope. "Risk."

"I like the way you say my name." He smiled.

"It's important that you stay awake tonight. In case of a concussion. You've taken a hard hit to the head."

"Tell me about it. It's pounding."

She jerked to attention. "How can I help?"

"Stay here and talk to me."

"I will."

"Good," he said, closing his eyes.

"But you have to stay awake."

He fought to open his eyes. "Then tell me more about my life, about us."

Oh boy, this wasn't what she'd expected, but what choice did she have? Was it so terrible for him to believe they were engaged for a short time, to give him peace of mind? She'd tell him the truth later, once he was feeling better. Right now, she had to keep him from dozing off.

She began slowly, giving him glimpses of his life as she knew it. She told him they'd met in high school but didn't get together until later in life—all true statements. She skimmed over facts, and thankfully he didn't ask questions but simply listened. Then she steered her one-sided conversation to his brothers and the ranch they lived on. She mentioned that Boone Springs had an annual Founder's Day party every year in town, honoring his ancestors and all the prominent people who'd contributed to the town. That big day was coming up soon, and all three of the brothers would be in attendance.

She knew a lot about the townsfolk, and so she kept a steady stream of information going, trying not to overload him with details but painting him a picture of Boone Springs.

"Does any of this sound familiar?" she asked, though she already knew the answer. She'd kept a watchful eye on Risk as she spoke, and there wasn't one sign, one spark of recognition registering on his face. So when he gave his head a tiny shake, she wasn't surprised.

"Let me check your wound," she said and rose up on the bed. She slid awkwardly across his body to garner a better look. She unwrapped the makeshift bandage, noting the lump on his head hadn't gone down. "Are you feeling any better?" she asked.

"My head still hurts a bit, but the rest of me is doing just fine."

She was inches from his face, and as she glanced at him, a small smile curved his lips and she caught his meaning loud and clear. When she'd first seen him injured, strong feelings had rushed forth. She'd cared for him, worried over him. He wasn't a stranger, but a man she might've loved if circumstances had been different. She hated what he'd done to her years ago, but she surely didn't want to see him injured again.

Risk had amnesia, she told herself, but that didn't stop her body from reacting to him, from tingling from head to toe, from turning her firm resolve into soft putty. With him smiling at her, his body granite hard, her defenses were down. And when he took her arms and stroked them up and down, drawing her closer, she didn't protest. She didn't back away.

And then his lips were on hers, gently, tenderly,

kissing her as if he was experimenting to see if he remembered something. He was so gentle, so deliberate, and every second was better than the next. His feathery kisses drew her in, every nerve ending awakened to the sweet pressure of his lips.

She needed to keep him awake and engaged…well—she had the engaged part down. As in, he thought they were. Now was her chance to stop him. To own up to the truth, to tell him it had all been a lie to prevent this very thing. Yet the words were not coming. How could they, when Risk was kissing her like this? Each kiss brought her a new kind of thrill. She'd never met a man like Risk before; she'd never felt this way about anyone else. Wouldn't Jenna Mae just die to find out her engagement ring plot had backfired?

"You're amazing," he murmured between kisses.

"Do you remember anything now?" she whispered.

"No, but I do know one thing. This feels right."

He laid another amazing kiss on her with his masterful lips. "Risk, maybe we shouldn't," she said softly between his kisses.

"My head is feeling better and better by the minute. Didn't you say I needed to stay awake?" He kissed her throat and nipped up to her waiting mouth. She was torn, confused, feeling helpless as the truth wouldn't come.

"Well, yes, but…you don't remember me."

"You've been caring and worried and well… I think I do know you. Somehow, I feel you with me. I see how compassionate you are," he said, taking her head in his hands. His eyes were bright and intense and goodness, he looked like Risk again, even with the bandage around his head. "And I'm certainly responding to you." He planted a beautiful kiss on her mouth and then paused. "Unless we haven't done this before? Have we? Tell me we have?"

"I, uh, yes," she whispered. "We've done this before."

"I need you, April. I need the connection."

She absorbed those words, and they touched down deep in her soul. She'd never reacted to any man the way she'd reacted to him. This Risk was sincere, genuine and sweet. This Risk was in need of more than sex, but intimacy, a bridge to his past. And today, she was it.

But could she discount her past with him? She'd been hurt by his actions, and he hadn't really made much of an effort to apologize to her. Her brain was telling her no, but her body was tingling all over and her big open heart was saying *yes, yes, yes*.

Only this time, she'd go in with caution, knowing not to have grand expectations. Could she be that woman who lived for this one night? Could she continue with the facade for just a little while longer? All the while knowing she would have to own up to the truth tomorrow?

She answered the question as her mouth pressed to his and she tasted him once again.

He touched her face, brushing a few curls from her cheek. "You're sweet and beautiful, April. I'm glad you're here with me."

"I'm glad I'm here with you, too," she said softly.

He kissed the words right out of her mouth. "No more talk."

"Is it hurting your head?"

"My head is not what's aching, sweetheart." His arms roped around her shoulders and he brought his lips down to touch hers in yet another kiss. April was at a loss to stop, and in the back of her mind she knew this would definitely keep him awake. He was definitely perked up now.

He might not know who he was, but he hadn't lost his finesse, and his near-naked rock-hard body was keeping her very warm. He stroked her arms and helped her remove her clothes. Then he began kissing the nape of her neck.

In the dimly lit room, he pulled the covers back a bit, exposing her body. There was admiration on his face, and deep desire. She was totally captivated by that look, by the reverent way his hands came to caress her breasts, as if in awe. She sighed at his intimate touch, her body trembling, her skin craving more from him. She was needy and ravenous and so taken by the attention he bestowed on her.

If he found her too curvy or lacking in any way, she didn't see it in his expression. She was at peace with her size and loved that he seemed to like her body just fine as well. He caressed her until tiny throaty sounds rose up from her throat, and then he moved lower on her torso and spread his fingers wide as he ran them down toward the apex of her thighs.

"Oh," she moaned once he stroked her center, and he smothered her cry with a deep lusty kiss.

* * *

Some time later, April lay beside Risk on the bed, her head on his chest. His arm was around her shoulders. "My head feels much better," he murmured.

April was glad about that, but she had to face facts: she was going to have to ruin all this bliss come morning, by owning up to her lies. She sighed and wished she'd never agreed to Jenna's plot in the first place.

"That's a good sign. I thought for sure you'd have a headache."

Outside the rain continued to fall, but with a little less force than before, and she wondered if the roads would clear or cell service would be restored soon. She doubted it would happen anytime soon. It was too risky for anyone to come out in such a torrential storm. The only saving grace was that Risk said he was feeling better.

"Well, I'd be lying if I said there wasn't a dull ache going on inside my head, but it's nothing I can't handle. Everything's a bit fuzzy." A growl rumbled from his stomach, and his eyes rounded in surprise. "Whoa," he said. "Guess I'm hungry. When's the last time we ate?"

"It's been a while. We didn't expect to get stranded in the storm, so what we have on hand is limited. But it's edible, and you should eat."

He nodded.

April rolled out of bed as discreetly as she could and quickly threw on her clothes. "You'll be okay here, right? I'll get us the food."

"I can go with you."

He made a move to get up, and she quickly put up

her hand. "No, please. It'll only take me a minute. Don't try to get up just yet."

He looked at her, debating, and then lowered back down against the pillow. "Okay. Be careful."

She almost smiled at that. He was telling her to be careful when he was the one who'd gotten injured. Yet it was sweet of him to be concerned.

He thinks you're his fiancée.

She dashed out the door and made her way to the kitchen. There on the table was the five-course meal she'd promised to conjure up in the form of muffins with peanut butter, apples and potato chips. She filled the thermos with water and then grabbed the food. As she made her way through the lobby, she picked up Risk's duffel bag and headed back to the bedroom.

She found him sitting up on the bed, staring out the window. "Dinner is served," she said, dropping his duffel and coming to sit on the bed beside him.

He looked at the food. "You really know how to impress a guy," he teased.

"I'm a master at making lemonade out of lemons."

"I can see that."

She handed him the thermos. "You must be thirsty."

"I am. Thanks." He put the thermos to his lips and took several gulps, then handed it to her.

She sipped from the thermos. "At least water is one thing we have in abundance."

Risk pointed toward the window. "Gross understatement, sweetheart." Then he plucked up a muffin and shoved half of it in his mouth. Chewing, he said, "These are pretty good."

"Your aunt Lottie made them. She's living on the ranch for the time being."

"Yes, you told me a little about her. So tell me more about you."

What could she say? That she had a fantasy crush on him and had for a long time, even though he'd done her wrong? That seeing him injured and vulnerable had stirred up her feelings for him again in a big way? That looking into his beautiful eyes made her do foolish things? Like pretending to be his fiancée. Like making love with him. "I was a chubby young girl and have struggled with my weight all of my life."

He shook his head as if he couldn't believe it. "You're…perfect, April. Just the way you are." He brushed his lips over hers tenderly, his assurance a balm to her soul.

"Thank you. I feel good about myself now, but I didn't always feel that way."

"Well, you should. Tell me more about you and your agency. How did you get into real estate?"

April told him more about her life, about her years in Willow County, about how her mother remarried and how she came to buy Bueller's antique store. She ended her personal history and shrugged. "Having my own agency is a dream of mine."

"It's weird—even though I don't remember, I feel like I know you. There's something pulling me toward you."

"You mean aside from the fact that we're stranded here in a pretty romantic setting."

He grinned and those hidden dimples popped out.

"I like the way you think, April. But yeah, it's more than that."

He grew quiet then, and she figured he was sorting things out in his head, or at least trying to. They spent time munching on muffins and chips and sharing both apples as the night wore on. "If you're still hungry, there's more chips and peanut butter."

"No, but what I am feeling is damn helpless." He swung his legs out from beneath the blanket. Before she could utter a word, Risk rose from the bed. He swayed a little but then righted his balance. She found herself staring at the back half of a buck-naked Risk.

Her mouth went dry watching the last of the embers cast light on his muscled form. "Are you okay?" she asked him.

"I think so. Feels good to get on my feet again."

He reached for the clothes she'd laid by the fire earlier and, with his back to her, gingerly put them on. She sighed in relief that he hadn't keeled over and that he wasn't naked anymore.

"This room is getting colder by the minute. Is there more wood?" he asked.

"Yes, but it's outside."

"How far?"

"By the front door. I only brought in what I could carry."

"I'll go get it."

"Risk, that's how you got hurt, going after firewood."

"The storm's letting up, and you said it yourself, it's only by the front door."

"Fine, but I'm going with you this time."

He walked over to her and put out his hand. "I'm good with that. Let's go."

After retrieving the last of the wood, Risk had restarted the fire in the master bedroom and now they were bathed in warmth once again. The small blaze was their only source of light tonight, since the lantern Risk had dropped outside when he was hit had probably been pulverized by the fierce winds. Once the fire died out, it would be dawn before they'd be able to see anything in the lodge.

But they'd made do with what they had and now both sat on the floor facing the hearth, letting the warmth seep into their bones. The rest of the lodge was freezing cold, but this room was like a sanctuary.

April rose. "I'll be back in a few minutes." She took some time to wash up and then soak a towel for Risk's head. When she came back, she spotted two foil-wrapped condoms that had magically appeared on the nightstand. Earlier Risk had been fiddling inside his duffel; he must've hit the jackpot, yet he hadn't said a word about it. They were just…there.

She didn't know how she felt about that. They hadn't actually had intercourse yet, but the night was long and they'd be sharing the bed. She knelt beside him and dabbed at his wound quietly as she mulled that over.

He grabbed her hand and ran his lips along her palm. "You take such good care of me," he whispered, gratitude in his voice. And then he lifted his head to look deep into her eyes. "You're amazing, April. You're the only real thing I know about myself." He pulled her close so that her leg brushed over his thighs and she sat straddling him. A groan rose from his throat and he cupped her head and covered her mouth with his. Teasing her mouth open, he thrust his tongue against hers in kiss after kiss. It was tender and sweet and hot all at the same time. She could kiss him all night long and never tire of it. Risk didn't hold back; he didn't temper or pace himself, and he certainly didn't seem unsure when it came to this.

It scared her a little that he'd put so much faith in her. That he'd accepted that she was his fiancée so easily, that she was the one thing he could count on in his world without memories. She'd wanted to tell him the truth, but his assumptions had been the only brightness he'd had. And resisting him at that moment hadn't been an option for her. Tomorrow would be soon enough, she told herself.

Suddenly, he stopped kissing her. "April?" She opened her eyes to the firelight dancing in his. "The fire's gonna die down soon, and there'll be a chill in the air. Maybe we should get into bed now."

She swallowed past her misgivings. She wanted this, wanted to be held and loved by Risk tonight. Unlike the last time, she knew nothing would come of it. "That's a good idea," she whispered.

Rising to his feet, he tugged her along, and they both climbed into the bed. He gave her the side closest to the fireplace.

His arms came around her to gather her up close, and with her back to his chest, she finally relaxed.

She liked being held by Risk, liked the safety he presented, the warmth of his body against hers. Today had involved a crazy set of circumstances: the storm, racing to the cottage, Risk losing his memory. Now that they were in bed together, a sense of peace stole over her, which was crazy, because they were low on food and had no idea what the morning would bring.

Cocooned by his strong body, she fell into the cadence of his breathing. She felt one with him and absorbed that feeling with each beat of her heart. But minutes later, when she thought he might have fallen asleep, his lips pressed against the nape of her neck and everything relaxed in her body suddenly jolted alive. She gave her approval with a sigh that Risk picked up on immediately. His hand came to the top of her rib cage, and his fingertips teased the underside of her breast. She ached for his touch, for him to continue his pursuit, and he didn't disappoint.

Effortlessly, Risk helped her off with her sweater and unfastened her bra. Then his hands were on her, and it was thrilling having him caress her in such a reverent manner, as if she were solid gold. Her body heated to a beautiful flame that Risk stoked with kiss after kiss. And then he turned her to face him and brought his mouth to her breast, moistening it, bringing the tip to a pebbled peak.

She was eager to touch him as well, and as she fumbled with the buttons on his shirt, he helped her lift it over his head. Then her palms flattened on his powerful chest and she kissed her way up his torso, her lips on his hot skin. And then their mouths melded again, the kiss fiery and frenzied, and they both groaned, rocked by the impact. They were equal partners: when he gave, she took, and when she gave, he took.

"I found protection, sweetheart," he murmured between kisses.

"Thank goodness," she whispered softly.

Seconds later their clothes were off and Risk was sheathed. She was ready for him, her body dewy and welcoming.

His lips came down to crush a kiss to her mouth at the same time he moved inside her. Sensations rocked her, her body recalling the feel of him, the fullness and total thrill. "Are you good?" he asked before thrusting again.

"So good."

He shifted, and his body covered hers. She kept pace, each thrust exciting her more and more.

Risk took complete control, and she followed him, her body in sync with his, her heart nearly bursting from her chest, her breathing hard and fast. He seemed to know what she needed, when she needed it, and soon she found herself melting, her body giving way, her world going up in flames.

"Risk," she cried out.

And then she splintered, shattered. Her entire body combusted, and Risk was there to catch her as she floated down. His kiss held promise, and she was ready for him, ready to give back all he'd given to her. It didn't take long for Risk to follow, his face a mask of pleasure as he made that one last final thrust. And it was an amazingly wonderful thing.

* * *

In the early morning, Risk rose and dressed quietly, then placed a soft kiss on April's forehead as she slept. He might not know anything about himself, but he did know he was damn lucky to have found a woman like April to love. She was caring and fun and beautiful with those long curly locks and bright blue eyes. She'd been extremely attentive to him and tried her best to encourage him, even though his mind was like a blank chalkboard ready to have the memories filled in. At least he had April to chalk in some things, and that had been a big help. He'd connected with her on many levels, but their time in bed was off-the-charts good.

While he didn't want to disturb her sleep, he was curious about the lodge and wanted to explore a bit. Without a sound, he made his way out the door and down the hallway to the lobby area. There he checked out the floors and walls, looking for any permanent storm damage, and then checked out the big triple-wide bay windows. Outside, the rain was down to a drizzle, which was encouraging.

"Risk?"

He turned to find April in the doorway, her arms folded across her sweater. "April, you're cold. Come here," he said. "I'll keep you warm."

She walked over, and he folded her into his arms.

"I woke up and you were gone. I didn't know if you were feeling okay or not," she said.

"Don't worry about me, sweetheart. I've got a hard head. Empty, but hard. I didn't want to disturb your sleep."

"You mean like you did last night?"

He laughed. Round two had been just as inspiring as the first time. Neither of them had gotten a lot of sleep, April doing her best to keep him awake. In the morning, she'd finally fallen asleep, and he might have dozed some, too. He was pretty sure he didn't have a concussion. Being with April was the best balm to his soul. She was his connection to his real life, not the one he'd had for less than twenty-four hours. "Hey, I didn't hear any complaints at the time."

She smiled. "No, no complaints."

He hugged her tight.

"So why'd you get up so early?" she asked.

"I got curious about the lodge. I mean, that's why we came here, right? You're my Realtor, and we need to check it out and see if it's a worthy investment."

"Yes, that's right."

"So, you want to do that?"

"Sure. Let's do it."

He took April's hand, and they finished up in the lobby, noting that a few of the rocks in the fireplace were loose. But the floors were in good enough shape, just needed a little TLC, and the windows were well insulated.

The kitchen was another matter. "The tiles are chipped so the counters would have to replaced and updated." He opened a few cabinets and checked inside. "A few of these are coming off the hinges, but the actual structure is sturdy. They'd need a little refurbishing— maybe a face-lift," he said. He looked at April. "Do the appliances work?"

"They do. For the most part." April made a face. "You don't think the kitchen needs to be gutted?"

"It's salvageable. There's a certain charm about this big kitchen. I think it could work."

"Really?" April smiled. "I'm glad you think so."

They walked into the dining area next to the kitchen. "This room seems solid," he said, looking around.

"And on a nice day, those windows bring in lots of light—you can see Canyon Lake from here," she said. "It's really a beautiful view."

"I bet."

"And we already know the master bedroom is good to go."

"Yeah, we do know that."

"I'm afraid the second floor isn't in as good shape. I mean, it is, but some of the rooms sprouted leaks from the storm."

As they climbed the stairs, she filled him in on the history of the rooms, the brother and sister team who couldn't quite get their act together. It didn't make any sense to him, but April seemed optimistic about the place. Her passion only endeared him to her more. This was important to her, and he didn't want to quell her enthusiasm.

"I know the roof needs repair," she said, "but if you decided to replace it, there's room for negotiation with the owner."

A sense of déjà vu took place in his head. It seemed as if he'd had this conversation before. It was only a flash, a snatch of a memory, or maybe he was just imagining it.

Still…it was encouraging. "You know something, I like this lodge. I see potential in it."

"I'm glad you think so." April beamed from ear to ear, and then a grumble rose from her stomach and filled the quiet room. "Whoa. Excuse me."

"Hey, I'm hungry, too. What do we have left?"

"Not much. Potato chips and peanut butter."

"You mean…breakfast?"

"Yes," she said, chuckling. "Breakfast. Washed down with a big gulp of water."

"Can't think of anything better."

She batted her eyes, and it was so adorable, he planted a kiss right smack on her mouth, the first real kiss of the morning. If he had his say, it wouldn't be the last.

Minutes later in the kitchen, he watched as April gently dipped chips into the peanut butter and set them out on the table as if it was a gourmet meal. He liked her style and her lack of panic in a situation that might've brought another person to tears. She'd taken control, mending him, trying to keep him from freaking out. Which, he wasn't gonna lie, was a battle. Not knowing anything about himself, his family and his past life was daunting. April filled the voids, but she didn't overload him with facts he'd have trouble processing.

With her by his side, he was sure he'd make it through any rough patches.

She set the thermos down between them, and together they munched on potato chips and sipped water. "Looks like the storm is letting up."

"Hopefully another one isn't on its tail. Maybe I should try to get to the car and see how bad it is."

"You mean maybe *we* should get to the car and see how bad it is."

"We?" He began shaking his head. "No, April. You said it's a mile to the car. And if another storm is coming, you shouldn't be out in it."

"If I'd gone with you for the firewood, maybe you wouldn't have gotten injured."

"Or maybe we both would've been. At least right now, one of us has their memory."

"The truth is, I don't want to be left alone in the lodge," April said, and Risk narrowed his eyes at her. She was nibbling on her lip, her eyelashes fluttering. Was she being honest? Was she really afraid?

"Okay, we'll stick together," he said finally.

A genuine look of relief washed over her face. Risk had made the right decision, but there were unknowns out there, and he would protect her like his life depended on it.

Early this morning, April had vowed to tell Risk the truth about their relationship. She should've done it the first thing, but then she'd found him exploring the lodge, and she'd gone along with it, losing her nerve. It wasn't an easy thing to admit, that they really weren't engaged *at all*, but she found him so charming and irresistible, she'd slept with him multiple times. How could she explain that away? And then how would she have explained the engagement ring on her finger? She didn't know what harm the truth would do to his recovery. Right now, she was the only bridge to his real life.

Yesterday, she'd been more concerned about his safety, seeing to his wound and taking that puzzled and fearful look off his face. Sharing a bed with Risk Boone to ward off the cold had been necessary, and he'd told her numerous times how much it meant to him that she was there with him.

But it was wrong to let him go on believing something that wasn't real.

Wrong to pretend they had a future.

If only it were true, because she was falling for him again.

And wasn't that a stupid thing?

She needed to tell him the truth. Today.

"You're not ready?" he asked, tossing his arms through the sleeves of his sheepskin jacket. "You need shoes and a coat, sweetheart. The rain's stopped. It's a good time to go."

"Oh, uh, I'll be ready in two minutes. And Risk?"

"Hmm?"

"When we get back, I need to speak to you about something."

"Fine. If we can't get the car started or find a way out of here, we'll have nothing but time to talk."

A few minutes later, they closed the door behind them and ventured out in the soggy murk that used to be the road leading up to the lodge. The air was fresh and cool, and it felt good to be outside after nearly twenty-four hours of confinement. Risk had a firm grasp on her hand, and the connection kept a steady surge of warmth flowing between them.

They sloshed slowly, taking cautious steps, fighting through strong breezes that rustled the trees and blew her hair in every direction. Her foot hit a dip in the road, and she stumbled, struggling for balance, but Risk was right there pulling her up before she fell. "Careful," he said, drawing her close. He bent his head and gave her a tender kiss on the lips. "Are you okay?"

She nodded, staring at his mouth, wishing for things that were impossible. "Yes, I'm fine. Thanks for the save."

"Any time," he said, his dark eyes gleaming.

This man, this Risk, was appealing and kind and…

Suddenly, a sound from above had both of them looking skyward—a *whop, whop, whopping* as a helicopter came into view. It flew directly over them, and as they lifted their gazes to the chopper, April recognized the Rising Springs Ranch logo immediately. "Risk, it's your family's helicopter. Looks like we've been rescued."

Five

Risk refused a gurney, but the Boone County Hospital staff who'd been waiting for him by the helipad insisted on putting him in a wheelchair. He grabbed for April's hand and she walked alongside him as he was wheeled to the back entrance of the hospital. Lucas Boone, who'd piloted the helicopter and flown them to safety along with Mason, walked a few steps behind their brother's wheelchair.

Cameras clicked away, and reporters eager for the scoop shouted questions. April recognized many of them. It surprised her to see them there, but then she'd almost forgotten how important the Boones were in this town. News of a Boone missing in a storm, even for one night, was sure to make headlines.

"Hey, Risk, how does this compare to the fall you took from Justice?"

"What happened to your head?"

April squeezed his hand, and he looked up at her, baffled.

"Can you make a comment, Mr. Boone? Give us something?" one of them asked.

Risk put up his free hand. "Hold up a minute, if you could," he said, turning to the nurse pushing him. The nurse looked none too happy as she brought the wheelchair to a halt.

Risk looked into the faces of the reporters. "I can't answer those questions. I don't remember. But I will say my fiancée took really good care of me when I got injured. April's been by my side the entire time, and we're both very fortunate we made it through okay."

"What do you mean, you don't remember? Do you have amnesia?" a reporter shouted.

"Are you saying you're engaged?" another reporter questioned.

Half a dozen more inquiries were shouted at both of them.

April froze as all eyes landed on her. She didn't have to see the look on Mason and Lucas's faces—they were behind her—to know they were in total shock about their brother's announcement. In less than a beat, cameras pointed her way and questions were hurled at her. She kept a stoic face, but inside her head was aching. Risk had just announced to all of Boone Springs that he had amnesia and that he was engaged to be married. A photographer bent down real low and snapped a photo of the diamond ring on her left finger.

By then, half a dozen hospital employees circled them, blocking the reporters from entering the building, and a doctor stepped up. "That's all for today. We won't know the extent of Mr. Boone's injury until we examine him. I know Mr. Boone would want you to respect his privacy."

"Does he have amnesia?"

"As I said, we won't know until we have a chance to give him a thorough exam."

Minutes later, Risk was brought into an emergency examining room. Lottie Sue Brown was waiting for him. His aunt Lottie was an icon around town, and even though April had never met her formally, she recognized her immediately from seeing her at local events.

Mason put a hand on Risk's shoulder, and Aunt Lottie bent to kiss his cheek. "You had us worried sick. We're all glad you were found safe."

Risk gazed at April, clearly baffled.

April whispered near his ear. "This is your aunt Lottie."

They'd been warned about his amnesia by a quick text from Mason giving them the information as April relayed it to him in the chopper. But Risk's total lack of recognition still seemed to come as a surprise to his family.

And needless to say, Mason and Lucas were eyeing her with extreme caution and curiosity after Risk's bold announcement that she was his fiancée.

Two ER doctors entered the room along with an-other nurse. "Please, I know you're worried about Mr. Boone, but we're going to ask you all to step outside now. We need to give him a thorough examination."

"Doctor, please let us know if you have any questions at all," Mason said.

"Of course." The doctor gestured toward the door.

Mason, Luke and Lottie filed out, while Risk held on to April's hand very tightly. She made a move to leave, and reluctantly, he released her fingers one by one. "I'll be just outside," she assured him.

He gave her a half smile as she exited the room.

As soon as she stepped into the waiting room, Mason, Luke and Lottie were waiting for her with wary looks on their faces.

Her stomach knotted into a tiny ball. She was in deep, almost wishing she was back at the lodge, away from the family, away from the media circus that would be her life unless she cleared things up.

Lottie was the first to speak. "Are you feeling all right, April?"

"Y-yes, thanks for asking. Other than feeling a little tired, I'm fine." She was drained, and not only because she and Risk had spent countless hours together, making love, keeping warm, staying awake out of fear of a concussion. The entire ordeal had been emotionally draining. How was she going to explain away the facts of the past twenty-four hours?

"Risk sang your praises," Lottie said. "You've taken good care of him."

"I tried my best." Her cheeks burned now.

"And is it a figment of Risk's imagination that you two are engaged?"

Once again, all eyes went to the ring on her finger. "Not exactly."

"What does that mean?" Mason asked, clearly puzzled.

Luke ran his hand across his forehead. "I'd like to know, too."

April closed the waiting room door and sat down. The rest of them took a seat, and she steadied her breath and garnered her courage. "We're not really engaged, but Risk thinks we are," she said, gauging their reaction. Her statement only puzzled them more. "You see, before Risk lost his memory, he thought I was engaged. I wanted him to think that for reasons I won't go into now. But then when I found he had a head injury and had lost his memory, I feared he had a concussion. I knew I had to keep him awake while I tended to his wound. I knew he couldn't fall asleep. He was weak, his brain foggy. But when he saw the ring on my finger and instantly assumed we were engaged, his whole demeanor changed and brightness entered his eyes. He saw me as a bridge to his life. I should've denied it then, I know that, but he seemed to really need the connection. And in the moment, he was relieved and happy."

While the brothers stayed silent, Lottie spoke up. "It must've been frightening for you. Being all alone in that deserted lodge with an injured man and a storm raging outside."

"It was, but thanks to the care package you made up, we had food to sustain us."

Lottie smiled warmly. "The boys think I baby them."

"It's a good thing you're so thoughtful," April said. Her shoulders slumped. All of a sudden, the adrenaline she'd been running on took a nose dive, and exhaustion set in.

"You said before he lost his memory, you told Risk you were engaged. I take it that's not true?" Mason asked.

April blushed.

"Mason, I think April needs to rest right now. She's clearly been through enough."

"No, no," April said. "I want to explain. I need to tell Risk the truth, too, but—"

"Maybe now's not a good time," Lottie said. "I think they'll be running a lot of tests on him, and he'll be too tired after all this."

"I agree. But I want to hear what you have to say," Luke said.

He'd been their savior, the man who'd rescued them from the lodge. She owed the Boones the truth, and she wanted to clear her conscience. She hated the pretense, all of it. Now, acid spilled into her belly as she began. "If I tell you now, will you promise to let me be the one to explain it to Risk once the doctor gives the okay?"

All three of them nodded.

"But only if you're up to it, April." Lottie really was a very nice person.

"I'm up to it. I just don't want to lose my nerve. You see," she began, choosing her words carefully, "Risk and I have some history together. We met shortly after his breakup with Shannon. And, well, it didn't end well with us, either, but there was an attraction between us, so my friend concocted this silly idea for me to pretend to be engaged while doing business with Risk. As an…insurance policy, if you know what I mean." She narrowed her gaze on the three of them, hoping they'd understand.

Again, they nodded.

"That's about it." Without going into details. "I wanted to keep things purely professional with Risk."

"Which didn't happen, I take it," Mason said, one brow arching.

"Shush," Lottie said. "That's between your brother and April."

She felt her face flame. She was not about to respond to Mason's question. This was all so very hard to admit, but at least she'd gotten it out without faltering. "For what it's worth, I'm sorry about all of this."

"It's not all your fault," Lucas said.

"You couldn't predict the storm would do so much damage," Lottie added.

"You helped my brother when he needed it most," Mason said, his mouth twisting a bit. "We'll always be grateful for that."

Though they said the right things, she got the feeling the Boone brothers were not thrilled about her lying to their brother.

"Yes, that's right," Lottie said. "You took good care of Risk, and now it's time you take good care of you. April, it's going to be a long night. Why don't you go home and get some sleep?"

"Shouldn't I stay and wait for Risk? He's a bit disoriented."

"We'll tell him you really needed your rest. He'll understand. I'll keep you posted, I promise. Mason has your number. Our car will take you home now, if you'd like?"

"That's very nice of you."

Lottie wrapped her arms around her shoulders in a much-needed hug. Lottie was astute, and April appreciated the kindness she bestowed on her after all that had happened. "You've been through enough today. Let me walk you out."

Mason and Luke nodded their goodbyes to her. Lottie stayed by her side, making sure April got into the limo, telling the driver to see her safely home.

And once April reached her home, she called Jenna Mae. "Thank God, you're home, Jenna. I really need to talk to you."

"Are you kidding? It's all over social media already. I'm listening. Tell me everything" was Jenna's reply.

April pushed the Off button on her cell phone after her long conversation with Jenna. Her friend always knew what to say, how to make sense out of things that really didn't make much sense. She loved both Jenna Mae and Clovie like sisters and didn't know what she'd do without them.

She took a bath, got into her coziest pajamas, made hot cocoa, which she hadn't touched yet, and tried to push the Off button in her head. "Damn."

It wasn't working. The past twenty-four hours

kept replaying over and over again in her mind. April couldn't pretend to be engaged to just anybody. No, she had to pick a nationwide rodeo and television celebrity. News of Risk Boone's sudden engagement was all over the internet, and there was no going back. She could only imagine the newspaper headlines in the morning.

Her cell phone vibrated on the coffee table, and she nearly jumped out of her skin. *He* was calling. Risk. The guy she'd lied to over and over again.

She reached for her phone, her hand shaking. "Hello."

"April, it's me."

"R-Risk, I didn't expect to hear from you tonight. How are you?"

"I'll be better once I get out of here. I've been poked enough for one day, and I'll have more of the same tomorrow. They're checking me out down to my toenails, but I wanted to make sure you're doing well. I…miss you."

April bit down on her lip. "I know, and I'm sorry I left the hospital. Your aunt insisted that I get some rest."

"She was right. You've been through a lot, too."

"How's your head? Are you in any pain?"

He sighed. "I'm doing okay. There's some slight swelling on the brain still. The doc says if I have a good day tomorrow and all the other tests are normal, I'll be going home the following day. Seems weird calling it *home* when I don't remember the ranch or my family."

"But maybe seeing it and being surrounded by your loved ones will spur your recollection."

"That's what the doctors are saying. The only memories I have are of you and me at the lodge." His voice took on a deep rasp. "I wouldn't trade those for anything."

"Yeah."

"You'll come by tomorrow, right?"

"Y-yes, I'll come by." She'd stop by the hospital for a quick visit, but she wouldn't confess to him until he got a clean bill of health from the doctors. Until that time, she'd just have to go along with the ruse.

She wasn't looking forward to revealing the unholy truth to him. Yet she wanted to be there for him because he needed her, and wasn't that just crazy? He still thought they were engaged, and *that* Risk, the sexy, sweet man she'd known after his injury, called to her. *That* Risk was a nice guy, and her soft spot for him had grown into a crater full of marshmallows. "I'll see you tomorrow, Risk. Sleep well."

"You, too," he said. "Good night."

She hung up and stared at the phone.

It wasn't going to be easy hurting him. And what effect would learning the truth have on his recovery?

The next day, April walked into Risk's hospital room holding a vase of colorful flowers. He was lying in the bed, his head against the pillow, his eyes closed. She was about to walk out of the room to let him rest when suddenly his eyes popped open.

"Hi," he said quietly, a smile on his face.

"Risk, I'm sorry. I didn't mean to disturb you."

"You didn't. You're the best thing that's happened

to me today. I've been waiting for you. Come closer," he said, gesturing for her to sit near him on the bed.

"Uh, first let me put these down." She set the vase on the table beside his bed and stood there, not sure what to do next.

"The flowers are nice, thanks. You look beautiful today."

She wore a short jean jacket over a blue floral dress. It was nothing terribly special, but she'd dressed up a bit for this visit. "Thank you."

He reached for her hand, and she stared at him a moment before locking fingers with him. He gave a little tug, and she was propelled forward, her knees touching the bedrail. "It's good to see you, April."

"It's good to see you, too. Still…nothing?"

"No, but seeing you makes it all seem okay." He stared at her lips, his eyes twinkling. "I think I need a kiss from my fiancée."

April blinked. She'd expected this, but it rang so false right now. She bent her head and gave him the tiniest kiss on the mouth. He wouldn't have expected anything less than that, and she wasn't going to give him any more. Just as she was backing away, the sound of heels tapping the floor had her swiveling around. And she came face to face with auburn-haired, green-eyed, perfect-size-two, classically beautiful Shannon Wilkes.

April couldn't believe her eyes. She stared at the woman for a whole five seconds before words could form. But it didn't matter. The woman wearing high-heeled boots, skintight black leggings and a sleek sage-

and-black belted tunic gave April a dismissive glance as she made her way over to Risk's bed.

A keen sense of déjà vu set in—the overweight girl of her youth felt invisible again.

"Risk, I came as soon as I heard. I'm so sorry about your injury. After how good you were to me when Mama passed last week, I had to come see you."

Risk shifted his attention to April, his expression blank. April was still stunned that she was in the same room with Shannon Wilkes, breaker of Risk's heart, among other things. And then it all became clear as she started putting two and two together. So, it was Shannon's mother who'd meant a lot to Risk. It was Shannon's mother who'd died. He'd gone to see Shannon when her mother was dying and had stayed for the funeral.

"I'm sorry to hear about your mother," Risk said. "But do I know you?"

"Of course you know me."

"Sorry, but I don't remember you."

Shannon's demeanor changed, her lips forming into a pout. "I'd heard about your amnesia on the news, but I wasn't sure if it was true. I didn't think you'd… you'd forget me."

As if no one in their right mind could ever forget such a super-duper star. The devil in April thought that was one good thing to come from Risk's amnesia: he'd forgotten the pain this woman had caused him.

"Sorry, but it's true. I don't remember you."

Shannon batted her eyes and turned to her, baffled. "You must be April."

"Yes."

"Shannon," she said, and then turned back to Risk. "I thought maybe if we talked a bit, privately, you might remember something about our past."

Risk turned to April, gesturing for her to come closer, and she went to his side. He reached for her hand and squeezed it. "I don't think it'll work. I mean, if my own fiancée can't jar my memory, I don't think you'll be able to." He entwined their fingers and kissed the back side of her hand. Shannon took it all in, her eyes flashing for a second.

There was loud commotion on the street, and April glanced out the third-floor window. "News vans are pulling up."

"Sorry," Shannon said on a shrug. "I tried to be inconspicuous and didn't tell a soul I was coming to see Risk."

Inconspicuous? With that face? In that outfit? She had to know that her coming to Boone Springs would create a media frenzy. It appeared she hadn't tried too hard to conceal her identity. She had one of the most recognizable faces on the planet right now. Sure, her recent love life had tanked almost as badly as her last movie, but she still had fans across many continents, and the camera loved her.

"I traveled a long way to see you, Risk."

"Are you famous or something?"

A wry chuckle escaped April's mouth.

"Yes, or something. But I came because we're friends now. You were so sweet to my mom, and you helped me so much during that time. And, well, you said if I ever needed anything, to come see you. Then I heard about your injury and, well, here I am."

Risk gave her another blank stare.

"Congratulations on your...on your engagement," she said, smiling at him. Then she turned to April. "To both of you."

"Thank you," April managed to say.

"It's funny, though. The entire time Risk was in Atlanta, he never spoke of being engaged."

Heat rose up April's neck. The woman was staring at her, and it was all April could do to keep her expression steady.

"I'm sorry, I don't have an answer for you," Risk said.

April kept her mouth clamped shut.

Two nurses walked in, one holding the biggest bouquet of exquisite red and white roses, both completely awestruck seeing Shannon Wilkes in person. The nurse set the vase on the table next to April's vase, and the overflow of roses completely drowned out her smaller bouquet. "Those are from me, Risk." Shannon smiled his way.

"Thank you," he said, uncertainty in his voice.

"Sorry to interrupt," one of the nurses said, her voice full of reverence. "But Mr. Boone is scheduled for more scans and tests this afternoon. We're going to have to ask you both to leave."

"Of course." April jumped to attention fast. She wanted out of this conversation. "I'll be going."

She pulled her hobo bag over her shoulder. Risk's gaze snapped to hers, regret in his eyes. It was clear he wanted a longer visit with her. She walked over to him and gave him a peck on the cheek.

Shannon seemed to home in on their interaction. "I'm staying at the Baron and planning on a long visit." She walked over to Risk and gave his hand a squeeze, gazing deep into his eyes. "You may not remember it, Risk, but you told me after Mama died to get away to clear my head, find out what I truly want in life. You invited me to your Founder's Day celebration, and I thought I'd have an extended stay in Boone Springs."

She had to be kidding. With the media surrounding her at every turn, peace and solitude would be the last thing she'd find in this town. Maybe Shannon was after more than a short respite.

Maybe she was after her hunky ex-boyfriend Risk Boone.

Six

Just after noon the next day, flanked by Mason on his left and Lucas on his right, Risk was taken in a wheelchair to the back entrance of the hospital. He'd gotten a clean bill of health: no concussion, no more swelling on the brain, no dizzy spells. They'd ruled out any health risks, and his tests had all come out normal. Yet he didn't feel normal, not when chunks of his memory had vanished. He was living in a vacuum; people knew him, but he couldn't remember them.

Shannon Wilkes was obviously a woman with a presence. She commanded attention with her style and manner. She had charisma, but he couldn't recall a thing about her.

"There'll be some reporters out there, so be prepared," Luke said. "You don't have to talk to them. Just get into the car and we'll do the rest."

"Am I really all that?"

"Yeah," both his brothers said simultaneously. "And your ex showing up here yesterday didn't help. Wherever Shannon goes, the paparazzi follow."

"You were nationwide news a couple of years ago, and now you're back in the news," Mason said.

Risk shook his head. "I don't get it."

"It's the life you led before you came back to work at Boone Inc."

"April told me some about my life on the rodeo circuit."

At the mention of her name, Mason and Lucas gave each other nervous glances.

"What'd I say?" he asked.

"Nothing," Mason was quick to respond. "April's coming by the house later on."

"Good, can't wait to see her."

This time the other two men stared straight ahead, zipping their lips. He wondered what was going on. Was this as weird for them as it was for him?

Risk wished April was here. She'd make this transition easier for him. But his neurologist had said not to overdo it on his first day, just to have family accompany him home. The doctor had already gone over the rules. Even though he was being released from the hospital, he still needed to take things slowly. Rest was important and so was seeing familiar things. And his fiancée was the most familiar thing he knew.

"Okay, it's showtime," Mason said as they approached the double glass doors. Half a dozen reporters were waiting, along with photographers lifting up their cameras. "Are you ready?"

Risk nodded and stood up. "Yeah, I'm ready."

The automatic doors opened, and Risk braved the onslaught of photos snapped and questions hurled at him while Mason and Luke ran interference, ushering him into the limo safe and sound.

"Go," Mason said, and the driver took off.

They managed to get out of the parking lot without incident, and as they made their way out of town, all of them relaxed. "Man, I don't know how you did this all the time when you were dating Shannon," Mason said.

"It's hard to believe I dated her."

"You did, for two years."

He shook his head, not recalling her at all.

"It's old news now. Don't worry about it," Luke said. "Hey, Aunt Lottie just texted me. She's making you your favorite lunch, Risk."

Risk scoured his memory, but nothing came to mind. "And what would that be?"

"Oh, sorry," his younger brother added. "Hickory-smoked steak sandwich with swiss cheese and crispy onions."

"Being that we were on a diet of peanut butter and potato chips at the lodge, that sounds damn good. I hope April comes in time to have lunch with me."

Mason slid a glance toward Luke when they thought Risk wasn't paying attention, but he picked up on it again. The secret looks were beginning to rub him wrong. What on earth was going on, aside from the obvious? "You gonna tell me why you're eyeballing each other every time I mention April's name?"

"We're not," Luke said innocently.

Mason shook his head like he was clueless, too, though Risk wasn't entirely convinced. He didn't know his brothers, so he wouldn't pursue it at the moment. Instead, he spent the rest of the time looking out the window, taking in the scenery, trying to conjure up a memory of the terrain, landmarks, anything at all that might spark a memory.

Nothing did.

April put her head in her hands as Jenna drove them through the gates at Rising Springs Ranch. It wouldn't be long now until she'd have to face Risk.

"Hey, April, you're going to be okay. It's the right thing to do."

She glanced up and turned to her friend. "I know. I've been rehearsing in my head what to say to him. I only hope I can get it all out before he kicks me out of the house."

"He wouldn't do that."

"I wouldn't be so sure of that."

"I'll wait for you, then. Or better yet, I'll go in and explain my part in all this."

"No, don't be silly, Jenna. This is all on me. I can do it. Listen, thanks for driving me. I really needed the lift."

"My pleasure. Besides, you left your car here."

"I meant the other kind of lift, too. You've been very supportive, and I appreciate that. You're the best."

"You'd do the same for me."

April smiled at her. They knew each other so well.

Jenna pulled the car to a stop in front of the house, and April leaned over and gave her friend a big squeeze. "Thanks for everything."

"You're welcome. Will you call me when you get back home?"

"Sure."

"Okay, go. Be brave. You can do this."

She nodded and exited the car, waving goodbye to her friend as she approached the front door.

The housekeeper answered on the first knock and ushered her into the big dining room. She stood on the threshold, feeling like an outsider. Mason, his fiancée Drea, Luke and Lottie were all sitting at the table poring over papers. She'd gone to grade school with Drea, and they were still casual acquaintances. April heard someone mention Founder's Day before all heads turned her way. "Hello, April," Lottie said. "Please come in."

She entered the formal dining that looked more like a Founder's Day war room. "Hello, everyone. I'm here to see Risk."

"Yes, about that," Lottie said, rising from her chair. "Let me give you an up-to-date report." Lottie took her elbow and gently guided her to the foyer by the staircase. "Risk is resting in his room. He's anxious to see you."

Her stomach squeezed into a knot.

"I spoke with his doctor this morning, and he's in pretty good shape, thank goodness," Lottie said. "And

I know you have to tell him the truth, but April, please do it in the gentlest way you know how. He's probably going to be upset. You're all he's been talking about lately. But he'll be able to handle it. Risk is tough, and I think the truth is always better than prolonging the lies."

"Yes, I agree. So I take it he still doesn't remember anything?"

"No, I'm afraid not."

"Okay, I'll do my best."

"His room is up the stairs, last one on the right. Would you like me to show you to it?"

"No, thank you, I'll find it."

"Okay," she said, giving her a sympathetic smile. "I'll leave you to it."

Lottie began to turn away. "Lottie? Can I ask you a question?"

The woman didn't hesitate as she faced her. "Of course."

"Why are you being so kind to me? I mean, I'm grateful that you are, but I wouldn't think I'm your favorite person right now, and you've been very understanding."

Once again, Lottie smiled, and her eyes twinkled. "Maybe because I've been in your shoes a few times in my life. We all make mistakes. We all make incorrect assumptions. Lord, we wouldn't be human if we didn't. And I see the way you and Risk look at each other. Mistake or not, I think there's a possibility of you."

With that, Lottie excused herself, and April took a moment to let that sink in.

There's a possibility of you.

No, there wasn't. April wouldn't even give that a moment of credence. She would try to straighten out this mess and then walk away from Risk and the sale of the lodge.

She climbed the stairs slowly, going over her rehearsed lines in her head, and then walked down the hallway and knocked on the last door to her right.

The door was yanked open, and there Risk stood, dressed in jeans and a blue chambray shirt, his dark hair slicked away from his face. Not even the stubble on his jaw or the small square bandage on his head could detract from how remarkably healthy he appeared. It wasn't what she was expecting.

"April, sweetheart. Come in."

Two strong arms came around her to encircle her body and nearly crush her to him. His lips brushed over hers several times, the sexy, delicious taste of him speeding up her heartbeats, making her yearn for more, almost making her forget her mission here.

Almost.

"Risk," she said, setting her palms on his chest. "We need to talk." Her command came out breathy and soft. Not at all how she'd intended.

"Talk," he said, "is overrated." He picked up her hand and kissed it, and then his mouth came down on hers again and again, kissing her so passionately her lips swelled. Then he pulled back. "But you're right. We do need to talk." He led her over to his bed, which looked as if it hadn't been slept in, and they both sat down. The bed faced a fireplace with a giant television screen over it. Shelves filled with Risk's rodeo trophies, champion buckles and awards lined one entire wall, and big manly pieces of furniture filled the large room.

"First of all, how are you feeling?" He continued to hold her hand.

"Me? I'm fine, really, but you're the injured one. How are you doing?"

"I still don't remember my family. Or this place."

"You…don't?"

"No, but I feel so much better now that you're here."

"That's what I wanted to talk to you about."

April rose from the bed and walked around to the footboard. Putting distance between them was essential to making her confession.

"Sweetheart, is something wrong?" There was alarm in his voice.

"No. I mean, yes. I have something to tell you. But first I want you to know that none of what I did was meant to hurt you. I, uh, haven't been exactly honest with you."

Geesh, this was harder than she'd imagined. He was looking at her like the fate of the world rested on her shoulders.

"This doesn't sound good." His voice lowered to a rasp, and the joy on his face faded.

"I can assure you, it all started out innocently."

"What started out innocently?"

"Well, not that innocently. When we first hooked up in Houston two years ago—"

"Hooked up?"

"Yes, we met there quite by coincidence, and we were together for one night. You see, you were heartbroken over Shannon Wilkes leaving you high and dry, and, well, I thought we might've had something, whereas you didn't. I spent the past two years not liking you very much. I know none of this is making too much sense. But when you came to me about buying the lodge, my friend thought it would be better to pretend I had a fiancé to keep things strictly professional between you and me, so that our past didn't interfere with our business relationship. That was working out well. Until you lost your memory."

Risk bounded off the bed and approached her. "I don't understand." His voice, a heartbroken rasp, churned her stomach. This was harder than she'd thought. "Are you saying we're not engaged?"

"Y-yes, that's what I'm saying."

"We were in the bedroom at the lodge."

"Yes, and you saw the ring on my finger and assumed we were engaged." She backed up a step.

"Are you saying you had sex with me when you were engaged to some other guy?"

"No, no, no. I wasn't engaged to anyone. It was all a…lie."

"And you didn't correct me about your phony ring?"

She shook her head over and over. "No… I didn't."

"You mean, you were in bed with me the entire night, letting me believe we were engaged? The things we did to each other, the way our bodies fit, the little cries you made, all of that was fake?"

"No, not fake. It was real. At least in the moment it

was. Oh, I don't know." Tears welled in her eyes. "It's all so jumbled up in my mind right now."

Lines formed around Risk's eyes as he narrowed his focus on her. "So that night in the parking lot when we kissed, I wasn't imagining it. You were drawn to me. It was crazy good, but afterward you stuck the ring in my face and I couldn't get over how I'd mistaken your signals. Now I get it."

"I'm sorry, really sorry about that, too."

Risk's nostrils flared; his eyes were two hard black stones. If he was facing down a wild feisty bronco, he couldn't have looked fiercer. "You lied to me over and over."

"I'm sorry. I didn't mean for this to happen. I don't want to upset you now. Risk, try to understand. Try to calm down."

And then it hit her. "Wait a minute." She searched his angry face, saw the fury in his eyes. Her heart pounded hard as realization blackened her mood even more. "How do you remember what happened in the parking lot? That was before you got hit on the head."

Risk blinked. His cover was totally blown.

"You got your memory back, didn't you?"

He glared at her.

"You did. When?"

"Hell, all I had to do was walk into my bedroom today and see those damn trophies up on the shelf. It all came rushing back to lucky me. Everything. I remember it all."

"I don't believe this. You let me go on and on. I was trying to explain and apologize to you. And you let me do it. You wanted to see me squirm when all I wanted was to tell you the truth." April was blindsided. Just minutes ago, Risk had welcomed her into his arms and had kissed and caressed her. It had all been a game. A mean-spirited game to get back at her.

"Woman, you wouldn't know the truth if it hit *you* in the head. You've lied to me since the day I walked into the Farmhouse Grill."

"It wasn't like that."

"I know exactly what it was like. Remember, I was there. I wasn't some foolhardy man getting sucked into buying a lodge that was clearly falling apart. Yet, once I got hit on the head, you did your very best to seduce me into changing my mixed-up mind."

"What! You can't possibly believe that!"

"Oh, sweetheart, you don't want to know what I really think about you."

April's blood raced through her veins. She counted to three to keep from spitting vile curses at him. What Risk was accusing her of was dead wrong. "Listen to me. I did what I had to do to keep you alive. I didn't know the extent of your injury. I'm no nurse but—"

"But you sure as hell have a great bedside manner."

"Shut up, Risk."

He laughed right in her face. "Oh, that's rich. You act like you're the injured party when all I got from you was a pack of lies, tied in a neat little bow."

"What you did when I first got here today was a lousy trick," she said.

"And what you did to me wasn't? How on earth do you justify that?" He came to within inches of her face, so close that she smelled his musky scent, saw the dark anguish in his eyes. "April, you led me to believe I loved you. That we had a future together, and your sorcery under the sheets convinced me. Actions speak louder than words, and woman, you have the best moves in town."

Her cheeks blistered hot. "I don't have to listen to this. I'm leaving."

She brushed past him, but his hand came out instantly and he held her firmly on the upper arm. She looked over her shoulder at him.

"Not so fast."

"Let go of me."

He unclamped his hand. "Fine, but you're not leaving until we get something straight."

She sighed. She'd heard enough from him today. "What is it?"

"You made a fool out of me. And now the whole world believes we're engaged. It's all over the newspapers and internet. There's no way to explain it away. With Founder's Day coming up and all that goes into that, I can't bring this farce out in the open now. It would completely overshadow an event that is important to my family. Shannon being here just complicates my life even more. It's a reminder to all how she dumped me two years ago. So, sweetheart, you're going to pretend to be my fiancée until after Founder's Day. And there's no way you're going to refuse."

She hoisted her chin. "I most certainly can refuse. I'm not doing that."

"You owe me this." He came nose to nose with her.

"After all the lies you told. Which I still don't exactly get. But now we're in this together."

"No."

"Yes."

"No."

He sighed. "This can go badly for both of us. What do you think will happen to the Adams Agency when the truth comes out that you lied, pretended we were engaged and seduced me to get that lodge sold?"

"That's not how it happened and you know it."

"I'm not sure what I believe."

"You wouldn't do that," she said, not entirely certain what a vengeful Risk would do.

"I wouldn't have to. People would make their own assumptions. And honey, I'm not exactly thrilled about looking like a fool, first with Shannon and then you. The headlines would crush all the goodwill my family has worked so hard to achieve this year."

April thought about it a long moment. "What are you proposing?" She frowned. It was a lousy pun.

"That we pretend to be engaged until the hoopla dies down after Founder's Day. That's ten days away. Then, later on, we'll quietly break up. It's the only solution."

"And my agency?"

"No one will know the truth. You have my word."

"I don't like it."

"I don't like it, either, but we don't have a choice."

"What do I get out of it?"

"Your agency wouldn't get dragged into all this. Isn't that enough?"

"No, I want something else from you, and it's a deal breaker."

"Hell, I'm afraid to ask."

"I want one more chance with the lodge. I want you to see it the way I envision it. I need your promise you'll consider it objectively, without bad weather and other things getting in the way. And then we have a deal."

Risk's eyes sharpened on her as he thought about it. She held her breath, hoping he'd come around.

"Done," he said finally. "I'll take a look at it one more time."

"Fine." April let out the breath she'd been holding. She wasn't thrilled with any of this, but she couldn't chance bad publicity for her agency, and if she could get an objective and fair opinion about the lodge from Risk, that's all she could ask. Then she thought about Mason, Luke and Lottie. "I've confessed to your aunt and brothers about the engagement, but what else should we say to them?"

"My family has to know the entire truth. I won't lie to them. I regained my memory just a couple of hours ago, and they don't know yet. We're going to tell them…together."

"Oh boy."

"What about you? Who knows about your fake fiancée scheme?"

"My two best friends. They'll keep the secret."

"Are you sure?"

"Yep, they're as loyal as they come. But how do we explain our quick engagement?" So far, she and

Risk had been insulated from questions, but they were bound to come at a relentless pace once they made public appearances.

"We've been quietly dating for a few months and fell for each other quickly. That's all anyone needs to know. That part won't be hard. What will be hard is pretending to the outside world we actually like each other."

"Yeah, maybe I should get some acting tips from Shannon Wilkes."

When Risk frowned, April felt a momentary triumph. She'd cling to that, because she feared other victories would be hard coming.

Risk would see to that.

In the evening, Aunt Lottie poured Risk and herself steaming cups of coffee and offered up a batch of peanut butter cookies she'd baked just for him. He didn't miss the irony that he'd lived on peanut butter and potato chips during his time at the lodge, and it almost put a smile on his face. *Almost.*

The house was quiet now. After sharing the good news with the family that his memory had returned, his brothers had hung around most of the day but had taken off right after dinner. It was relaxing sitting here with his aunt, digesting the events of the day without a commotion.

"Too bad April couldn't stay for dinner." Aunt Lottie brought her cup to the table and sat down facing him.

"I think she's planning to avoid me as much as possible until this farce is over. She couldn't wait to get out of here today."

"Yet she agreed to your plan." Lottie sipped her coffee.

Risk grabbed two big cookies from the platter and set them on his plate. "She had to."

"Why? Did you pressure her?"

He chomped down on his cookie, chewing as he thought about the question. "A little. She got us into this mess. Now she's gonna have to be by my side until after Founder's Day. But only when absolutely necessary."

"It is messy, isn't it? Granted, I don't agree with her tactics, but she did take good care of you when you were injured, and for that we're all grateful."

He took a sip of coffee—the brew went down nice and smooth, unlike his aunt's comment. "You think I'm ungrateful?"

"You tell me. Are you?"

Risk was too steaming mad at April to admit she'd been instrumental in helping him when he'd been hurt. "No, not about that. But I can't get past why she found it necessary to lie to me, over and over, or why she concocted a story about her being engaged in the first place. I don't get it."

"Don't you?" Aunt Lottie's eyes twinkled a bit, and she smiled before taking another sip of coffee. "I think you can guess why she did it."

Risk wasn't going there. He couldn't possibly discuss having sex with April with his aunt. He couldn't tell her about their night in Houston and how he'd behaved afterward. Plus, that was then and this was now. And *now* he was pissed at April for making a fool out of him.

The sound of approaching footsteps and someone clearing his throat had them both turning toward the kitchen doorway. There stood Drew MacDonald, looking a bit sheepish, holding a bouquet of fresh yellow roses and a gold box of candy. "I hope I'm not interrupting. I wanted to pay you a visit, Risk. Heard about your accident."

"Hey, Drew, nice to see you. Come in and have a seat. You're not interrupting anything."

"Thanks." He walked over to Lottie first and handed her the flowers. "These are for you, Lottie. For baking me those delicious cranberry muffins the other day."

"For me? Why, they're beautiful." There was surprise in Lottie's eyes. "I, uh, assumed they were for Risk."

"Nope, Risk gets these." He handed over the gold box. "Mason told me they were your favorite."

Risk took a second to open the box and gaze at the dozen dark chocolate truffles in gold wrappers. "Yep, these are my favorite. Thanks, Drew."

"No thanks necessary. I'm glad you got your memory back. That must've been strange."

"You have no idea. Aunt Lottie, does Drew know how your muffins saved the day for us when we were stranded at the lodge?"

"I'm not sure he does," his aunt said, admiring the flowers, touching the petals. It was about time Drew made some headway with his aunt. They never seemed to be on the same page, but maybe now that Lottie was sticking around for more than a millisecond, the two would finally find common ground.

"She did. She packed a basket of muffins, protein bars and fruit for the trip to the lodge, and that food sustained us overnight. Aunt Lottie has good instincts."

Drew smiled at her. "I suppose she does."

Risk's cell phone rang. He took one look at the screen and then rose from his seat. "Drew, excuse me. I've got to get this."

"Sure, no problem. Go right ahead."

Drew watched Risk walk out of the kitchen, leaving him alone with Lottie. She immediately rose and walked over to a kitchen cabinet. "I'll just put these in water."

She opened the cabinet door and, standing on tiptoes, reached for a frosted glass vase.

"Here, let me help you get that." He came close to Lottie, his hip brushing her side as he retrieved the vase and set it down on the counter. He was as close as he'd ever been to her, and his heart began to race.

"Thank you," she said, gazing up at him. "These are very pretty, but they weren't necessary."

"You deserve them," he said, lifting a hand to her face. His fingers brushed her soft cheek. "I think I overreacted before and, well, I don't want a misunderstanding coming between us. We've been friends too long."

"I, uh, agree. But it was my fault for doubting you. When you lifted that bottle, I shouldn't have assumed you were drinking again. I jumped to the wrong conclusion, and I'm so sorry about that."

Ever since his wife, Maria, had died, he'd been battling alcoholism, nearly ruining every relationship he'd had. But he was clean and sober three years now, vowing to never go back and trying to make amends. Lottie's lack of faith in him had hurt his pride and blistered his heart.

"I've already accepted your apology. That happened a few months back and, well, I'm over it. Fact is, I miss seeing you."

"I've missed you, too, Drew."

"You have?"

She nodded, her eyes gleaming bright in invitation.

Drew bundled up his courage. "I've wanted to do this for a long time." He touched her cheek once again, bent his head and brushed his lips over hers. Lottie's mouth was soft and delicate. It'd been years since he'd kissed a woman. He was grateful she didn't pull away and call him a bumbling fool. When he finally did end the kiss, her eyes were still closed, and a sweet smile surfaced on her face, giving his heart a lift.

"Lottie?"

"Hmm, yes?"

"It's okay that I kissed you?"

She searched his eyes now and spoke ever so softly. "Oh, I think so, yes."

Something amazing filled him up now, and he wished he'd had the courage to pursue Lottie years ago. "Then I have a question for you."

"What is it?" she asked, her pretty eyes curious.

"Would you allow me to escort you to the Founder's Day party?"

"Oh yes. I'd like that."

Risk entered the room again, and they pulled apart immediately. Lottie grabbed the vase and filled it with water at the sink. Drew ran a hand through his hair. He was keyed into a dozen different emotions at the moment.

Risk didn't acknowledge he'd seen or heard anything, yet Drew still had a tough time looking Lottie's nephew in the eyes. And he supposed Lottie felt the same way.

But damn, the kiss had been good, so well worth the wait.

On Friday afternoon, April sat at her office desk making headway with her plans to stage the lodge for Risk's viewing next week. She'd contacted Mr. Hall and explained to him that the lodge needed a quick face-lift to spark interest. April planned on using many of her own home accessories to liven up the place. Since her return to town, her engagement to Risk Boone had stirred up revitalized interest in Canyon Lake Lodge. She'd gotten calls and answered questions about the lodge from a few potential buyers, and she'd made the owner aware of that. Luckily, Mr. Hall was a reasonable man, and he'd agreed to making some minor renovations.

She happened to glance up at the front door at the exact moment Shannon Wilkes walked into her office. April dropped her pen and gave Clovie a quick glance.

Her assistant's eyes widened, and she rose from her desk. Shannon was the last person April had expected to see walking through the office door. Then three news vans pulled up on the street, and April quickly rose from her seat, brushing past Shannon to walk over to the door and lock it.

"I'm sorry about that," Shannon said, smiling. Her auburn hair was tied up in a tight ponytail that highlighted her perfect bone structure and pretty face. "I can't go anywhere lately." She put out her hand. "Hello, April."

April forced a smile and took her hand. "Hello."

Shannon glanced over at starstruck Clovie.

"Shannon, I'd like you to meet Clovie. She's my right-hand woman here at the agency."

"Nice to meet you," her assistant said.

"Same here," Shannon said graciously, and then turned to speak to April. "Do you have a few minutes? I promise it won't take long."

"Well, I am sort of busy."

"Please." Shannon kept smiling at her, not flinching, not backing down. April had to admit she was curious about what Shannon would want with her.

She glanced at her watch. "Okay, sure. I have a few minutes until my appointment." An appointment that consisted of going to the hardware store to pick out paint colors for the lodge's mini renovation. But Shannon didn't need to know that. "Why don't you have a seat at my desk over there?"

She pointed to the chair, and Shannon eagerly sat. "Thanks."

April took her seat behind her desk, stacking up her notes and putting them out of view. "What can I do for you?"

"Well, first, how are you feeling after your ordeal?"

"I'm…great. No complaints. Thanks for asking."

"Aren't you thrilled Risk got his memory back?"

"Yes, thrilled." April gave a mental eye roll.

"I stopped by the ranch to see him yesterday, and he was back to his old self. I couldn't believe he didn't remember me at the hospital."

"No, well, that's what happens with temporary amnesia."

"So, we got to talking about this adorable little farmhouse I was on the verge of buying when Risk and I were together. We wanted a place to have some privacy, you know, when I'd come visit him here in Boone Springs. He did tell you about this, didn't he?"

All this was news to April. Of course, she wasn't the resident Realtor back then, but Shannon was leading up to something, and April wasn't getting a good feeling about this.

"Well, I, uh, we haven't spoken about this, no." She hadn't spoken to Risk since he broke the news to his family about their pretend engagement. She'd felt so awful that day that she'd gone home and binged on an entire bag of chocolate chip cookies. Which had only made her stomach ache even more.

"I drove past the place yesterday, and it's still so quaint and charming. I was hoping to find out if the home owner is interested in selling?"

"Do you have the address? I have potential listings for several charming little farmhouses on the outskirts of town."

Shannon dug into her cherry-red Ferragamo handbag and came up with the address. "Here you go."

April took a look at the address and checked her register. "No, that house isn't listed, so I'm assuming it's not for sale. That sale did take place some time ago. Sorry I can't help you."

"Oh, that's a shame. I was really in love with that place, you know, as a getaway. It's peaceful there."

"But is it for you?" April blurted. After Founder's Day she wouldn't care where Shannon took up residence, but she didn't want to have to deal with her now. And of all places a starlet might want to live, she couldn't believe Boone Springs would be high on the list.

"That's what I'm hoping to find out. Would you mind checking with the people living there, to see if they're interested in selling? I'd give them a more than fair offer along with a bonus if they are. Maybe you and I could drive out there and talk to them."

It was the last thing April wanted to do.

"Ah no, I can't do that any time soon, but I will give them a call and get back to you. Is that fair enough?"

"I suppose it'll have to be."

"Oh, and Shannon, is it always like this with you?" She pointed to the reporters milling around the street waiting for her to exit.

"Some days are worse than others. And coming here

to see you, Risk's new fiancée, might have something to do with it."

"You think?"

Shannon smiled.

April hated to believe the worst of people, but maybe Shannon's appearance in Boone Springs had more to do with her needing headlines and getting back in the public eye than anything else. Her last two movies had tanked at the box office. And presently she was unattached.

Shannon studied her a minute. "Thanks for your help today. I hope to hear from you soon."

"No problem, I'll call you. You're at the Baron, right?"

"Yes, I'm staying there. And don't get me wrong, the food at the hotel is fine, but I'm getting so darn tired of it. I was trying to remember the name of the Mexican restaurant Risk adores. They make his favorite meal there. Oh gosh, you must know the name of the place." Shannon gave her a pointed look.

"I, uh, you know, I'm forgetting the name of the place, too."

"Really? Gosh, Risk used to crave their food all the time."

April had no clue. There was so much she didn't know about her pretend fiancé. She rose from her seat. "Sorry to rush you, but I'm going to be late for my appointment if I don't get going. Let me walk you out."

Shannon rose, and they made their way to the front door. As soon as April opened it, cameras flashed and reporters started in with their questions. She backed away quickly and closed the door as Shannon met with her paparazzi.

April could only imagine tomorrow's headlines: "Risk Boone's Women, Then and Now."

Seven

April opened her apartment door on the second knock and faced Risk, standing there holding a bag of food from the Gourmet Vaquero. "You brought dinner?"

"I'm hungry, and when you called today, I got to craving these empanadas. Besides, I was followed by the press, so it looks good that I'm here, delivering my fiancée her dinner. Play along." He bent his head and kissed her boldly on the lips. Shock stole over her, and he murmured, "Guess you haven't taken any acting lessons yet. Better work on that. We're being watched."

She wasn't so sure they were—she didn't see anyone out there—but Risk wouldn't have kissed her otherwise. He'd made it clear what he thought of her.

She wrapped her arms around his neck, breathing in his scent, remembering a time when she thought it was sexy. She kissed him back, putting a good deal of pent-up emotion into the melding of their lips. For anyone watching from afar or snapping pictures, it must have looked like blazing passion instead of acute displeasure.

When the kiss ended, her heart was racing. Risk was staring at her as the seconds ticked by.

"Come inside," she said, so she could stop pretending she loved him—or liked him, for that matter. Yet her lips tingled and heat began rising up her throat.

He stepped into her apartment, and she immediately closed the door.

Risk ignored her sigh of frustration and scanned her place, approval gleaming in his eyes. April had a flair for design and color. She liked to think she had unique style in decorating. The front rooms in her apartment were furnished with varying pieces of contemporary furniture that lent a modern tone while still being warm and inviting. Risk was nodding his head as he took in the living-dining room. "Nice place."

"Thanks." She so wasn't going to give him a tour of the other rooms. "Listen, I only called you after Shannon left my office because I realized we don't know enough about each other to make this work."

"Yeah, you're right. It's not as if we could discuss this at a restaurant or anything. Besides, shouldn't a fiancé know what his girl's apartment looks like?"

That much was true. He'd never been here before.

"Okay, why don't you take a seat and get comfortable in the dining room. I'll get this meal on the table."

"I'll help," he said. "I don't expect you to wait on

me, unless someone's watching." His lips twitched again and she wanted to swat at him with a dish towel.

"The little woman catering to her man. Risk, I honestly don't know how you survived in this century with thinking like that."

He shot her an innocent-little-boy look, as if anything about Risk could ever be innocent.

She grabbed the bag out of his hand and headed to the kitchen. "Let me take a look at these world-famous empanadas." He was steps behind, and when she put the bag on the counter and opened it, the most amazing aroma drifted up. Her stomach growled. "Wow, those do smell good." She pulled out half a dozen wrapped empanadas, along with a smaller bag of chips and salsa.

"Wait until you taste them." Risk was practically salivating.

"Okay, so empanadas are your go-to food. And that Tex-Mex restaurant is your favorite. That's a start," she said. "When Shannon showed up at the office today, I was sort of stumped by her questions."

April handed him plates and utensils while she picked out two beers from the fridge. "This okay? I also have wine or soda."

"Beer's fine."

"The thing is, I don't get Shannon. She claims she wants a little getaway here in Boone Springs. I'm looking into properties for her, but I can't see it."

"She's impulsive. I don't think she'll follow through. She has trouble doing that." Risk was thoughtful for a minute, and she wondered if he still harbored feelings for his ex. But it was none of her business anymore. All she had to do was get through this week, then she'd be free of this ruse.

Risk put the plates out in the dining room, and she set the food on a platter. She placed it on the table and then handed him a beer as they sat down. "I'm amazed that you're friends now after all she put you through."

Risk frowned. "It wasn't always like this. In the beginning, I was pretty devastated."

She knew. That's when she'd spent the night with him.

"Then my hurt turned into indifference, and I realized Shannon wasn't the woman for me after all. But her mama was a special lady, and seeing what Shannon went through these last few months made me sympathize with her. I mean, I lost both my parents at a young age, and it was extremely hard. We're on friendly terms now, but I wouldn't say we're good friends."

"She thinks you are. She made a special point of letting me know she came to visit you yesterday. She's absolutely thrilled you got your memory back."

"Look, all I'm interested in is getting through this thing, and then all of our lives can go back to normal."

Risk put the bottle of beer to his lips, and his throat worked as he took a swig. She found herself staring, remembering how things were with them at the lodge after he'd lost his memory. That Risk, any woman would want to be friends with, or more. She cleared her throat. "Let's eat and get down to the bare facts," she said.

Risk took a bite out of a beef empanada.

She grabbed one of the pastries filled with chicken and Mexican spices. "Oh wow," she murmured softly as the flavors erupted in her mouth. "These are delicious."

"Right?" Risk smiled, and his entire demeanor changed.

They spent quiet moments filling their bellies, the food tasting too good to interrupt with any discussion. When they were done with the empanadas, they began munching on tortilla chips.

"What's your favorite flavor of ice cream?" she asked.

"Butter pecan, but I don't refuse any flavor of ice cream. What's yours?"

"Chocolate chunk brownie. Drink of choice?"

"Bourbon straight up and beer." He lifted the bottle to his lips. "Yours?"

"Green tea."

He rolled his eyes. "Alcohol?"

"Margarita. Baseball, football or basketball?"

"All of the above. I watch them all. I played baseball in high school. You?"

"I ran track in college and play tennis once in a while when I find the time. I like to watch football, of course."

And after they left the food and sports category, they dived into their early childhoods. "What was yours like, Risk?"

"Mine? Pretty good. I mean I have two pain-in-the-neck brothers, but we all got along okay. We had a lot of fun on the ranch, even though Dad worked us hard. But after my folks died in that accident, we had some difficult years. Luckily, we had each other. My father wanted us to know the business from the ground up, and my brothers were fine with picking up where Dad left off. But I always knew there was something out there for me more exciting then raising cattle and making business deals. I think I was at my happiest riding rodeo. I loved the excitement and thrill. I loved challenging myself."

"And the danger?"

"It's not all that dangerous if you know what you're doing."

She stared into his eyes, not bringing up his career-ending injury.

But he must've read her mind. "I was off my game that night I got hurt. Things weren't great with Shannon. We'd had a fight the night before, and, well, I guess I was distracted." He finished his beer and set the bottle on the table softly. "What about you?"

"Me? Well, I didn't have a great childhood. My dad left the family when I was six. He just up and took off, leaving me and my mother to fend for ourselves. Mom tried her best to provide for us. She worked two jobs, and I was home alone a lot. I guess that's when I started overeating. Before I knew it, I was at an unhealthy weight, and I realize now, I used that weight as a form of protection. It's hard being hurt like that, you know?"

Risk listened and nodded, softness touching his eyes. "Does your mom live in Boone Springs still?"

She shook her head. "Mom remarried five years ago

and lives on the East Coast now. She's been traveling Europe with her husband these past few months. He's a tech consultant and speaks four languages. My mom and I talk whenever we can. I think she's finally managed to put her heartache behind her and she's happy. That's all I wanted for her."

"What about you? Have you found what you're looking for?"

"Well, I'm living my dream, working in real estate, owning my own business."

"I meant about your love life?"

"Oh, I, uh…there've been a few men in my life."

"Anyone I should know about?"

She eyed him. "No one special, if that's what you mean."

"No one?"

She shrugged. Was it so hard to believe she'd never met a guy who made her heart sing? "I dated when I was in college, and that's where it ended. I never met anyone right…for me."

Why was she revealing all this to Risk? He only needed to know facts, not the emotions behind them, but once he opened up about Shannon, she felt a bit more comfortable speaking about her past. "Hey, how about we move on to music? What's on your Spotify right now? What do you like to see at the movies?"

They spent the next hour answering each other's questions, getting down to the basics. She took notes, and after they'd gone through a six-pack of beer, it was time to call it quits. She walked Risk to the door.

"I think this was a good idea," she said, feeling much more confident about her role as his fiancée now.

"Yeah," he said. "We managed to keep it civil."

"Yes. Good practice for when it's the real thing."

"Shoot. It almost slipped my mind. Our first test is coming sooner than I expected. We're invited to speak about Founder's Day at the elementary school tomorrow afternoon."

"We?"

"The principal asked for you to come specifically, and I accepted."

"You accepted? Really? You don't even know if I'm available."

"April, this week you're *always* available when it's necessary, and this is necessary. The principal thought you can speak about what living in Boone Springs has meant to you."

"But I'm not even prepared."

"They're grade-school kids. It won't be hard. Just wing it."

"Easy for you to say."

"Hey, a deal's a deal. And you agreed to all this."

He didn't need to remind her—she was well aware. "I was forced into this, remember? And next time, give me more than a half day's notice when I'm supposed to make an appearance."

"I'll email you the agenda of appearances ASAP."

"There's so many I need a list?" She wasn't happy about this.

He shrugged. "Thanks to our *engagement* and Shannon's visit to town, our dance card is filling up fast."

She walked him to the door. "You don't have to accept all of the invitations."

"I'm not, trust me. I'll pick you up tomorrow around ten."

She sighed. "I'll be at the office." Then she pointed a finger toward his chest. She didn't give a fig if the paparazzi were out there, stalking them. "And don't you even think about kissing me goodbye."

Risk's lips twitched, his eyes sharp and keenly aware. "I wouldn't dream of it."

With that, he walked out, and she gently closed the door before he could say good-night.

April stood next to Risk behind the podium in front of two hundred grade-school students sitting on the multipurpose-room floor of Creek Point Elementary. Risk had them captivated with his stories about how the town of Boone Springs came to be. He spoke of his ancestors with pride and passion and then brought his young audience up to date on what each of his family members had done to keep Boone Springs thriving. He was good with the kids, inspiring, even, which totally surprised her.

"And now, I'll turn the microphone over to my fiancée, Miss April Adams. She wants to tell you something about what Boone Springs means to her." Risk gave her a charming, melt-your-heart smile, and she tried to smile graciously back at him. As if she liked him.

"Hello, children. I'm April, and I grew up in Boone Springs just like many of you. But when I was young, this school wasn't built yet. I went to Brookside Elementary. Back then we only needed one grade school in the community and now we have three, so you can see how much we've grown in just over twenty years."

Eight teachers stood at the back of the auditorium, their gazes glued to her. The children, too, seemed to be listening, but it was Risk's eyes on her that rattled her nerves. He seemed intent on her every word. She'd taken his advice and was winging it.

"So when I moved away to learn all I could about real estate, my heart was always here in Boone Springs, where I grew up, where my family and friends were, and I worked very hard to come back here and open an office. *People* make Boone Springs special, people like you and your families. They work hard, too, and they give back to the community, by supporting the schools and libraries, by volunteering at the hospital and shelters, by helping their neighbors. Can you tell me what you can do to help the community, your neighbors and your families?"

Hands went up, and April called on a little boy in a red flannel shirt. "I can put my toys away when my mommy asks."

"That's very helpful." April grinned and nodded, then called on an older girl, whose gaze seemed to be fixated on her "fiancé."

"I want to be a doctor when I grow up."

"That's very helpful, too," April said. "There are all kinds of doctors. What kind would you like to be?"

The girl didn't hesitate. "The kind who helped Mr. Boone when he lost his memory."

The teachers all smiled, and Risk's lips twitched but he had the good grace not to chuckle, like some of the child's schoolmates were doing. "Yes, the doctors who helped my, uh, Mr. Boone, were quite competent, and we're very grateful." She turned to meet Risk's eyes and found softness there. He was a better actor than she was.

Once the assembly was over, Risk and April thanked Mr. Ritter for the opportunity to talk to the kids. But when the principal seemed in no rush to end the conversation, Risk took hold of April's hand and squeezed. "Sorry to rush off, Mr. Ritter, but we've got another appointment this afternoon."

"Of course," he said. "Thanks again. Both of you were great. The kids learned so much from your talk. And Miss Adams, you did a wonderful job in engaging the students."

"She's an amazing woman," Risk replied and then began walking out of the auditorium, tugging her along.

Once in the parking lot and away from curious eyes, April let go of his hand. Risk opened the car door for her, and as they both took their seats, she turned to him. "I hope you weren't serious about us having another appointment this afternoon. It wasn't on the agenda."

He turned on the engine and buckled up. "I'm serious…about lunch. I'm starving."

"Well, you can eat. Just drop me off at my agency first."

He only smiled. "Sorry, can't do that. The place is around the corner from here."

"Risk, if I'm so horrible, why would you want to spend more time with me than necessary? Because I certainly think you—"

"April, I'm hungry, and it'll only take a few minutes to get the food and eat it. We don't even have to talk to each other."

She folded her arms across her middle. "Fine then."

Risk wasn't fooling; the Thai Temple was indeed just a few minutes away. He drove up to a take-out window and ordered two meals. They were cooked fresh, the scent of sizzling meats making her tummy grumble when Risk was handed the food in two white bags. "You like Thai?" he asked.

She nodded, though she hadn't tried this place. It was relatively new, she assumed, since this part of town, including Creek Point Elementary, had been recently developed.

He drove out of the drive-through heading in the opposite direction of her office. "Where are you going?"

"You'll see. There's a park on the edge of town. We're almost there."

It did no good arguing with Risk. He was determined to have his lunch on his terms, so she clamped her mouth shut as he turned into a dirt driveway and parked the car. He turned to her. "Walnut shrimp or glazed chicken?"

She stared at the two bags and took the walnut shrimp. "This one is fine."

He nodded, grabbed the other bag and got out of the

car. He walked around to her side and pointed. "There's a table over there, looks out to the creek. That's where I'll be," he said, sauntering away. As an afterthought, he turned to look her square in the eyes. "You comin'?"

Then he headed over to a table set under a stand of trees. She stubbornly sat in the car and watched Risk take a seat at a wooden picnic table. She looked out at the annoyingly lovely view. The sun blazed over the ridge as waters from the recent storms rushed along. It was a far better place to have a meal than in the car. She hated that good sense won over her stubbornness. She opened the door, bag in hand, and walked over to the table.

Risk didn't say a word. He was busy eating and enjoying the view of the rocky bed and bubbling waters.

She opened her bag, stirred the shrimp, rice and veggies together, and began eating. The food was spicy and delicious, and she dug in with gusto.

Risk glanced at her. "You're a noisy eater."

"Am I disturbing your peace?"

"Always," he said. "As I recall, you're noisy about other things, too."

Heat rose up her neck. Was he deliberately taunting her and trying to humiliate her? She'd been hijacked into this lunch, but she didn't need to be insulted as well. She rose from her seat. "This wasn't a good idea."

"Hell, April. Why are you being so sensitive?"

"Because you're bringing up something I want to forget."

"You know darn well it wasn't meant as a put-down."

"I know no such thing." Because if it wasn't a put-down, then what was it? He had good memories of the night at the lodge? He liked the sounds she'd made while he was making love to her? None of it mattered; none of it was real. She hated the deception and didn't want to spend any more time with Risk than she had to. "I'm done here."

She marched off, heading toward his car. When she was halfway there, Risk sidled up next to her, took her hand and twirled her to face him. He came nose to nose with her and whispered, "Don't look now, but we were followed."

"What? Where?"

He touched her cheek with the flat of his palm. "Over by the side of the road. They're taking pictures."

"Oh. Who are they?"

"Reporters, no doubt. It looks like we're fighting."

"We are."

"Not anymore," he said softly, bringing his head down, touching his lips to hers. The kiss startled her, but he held her tight around the waist, keeping her in his embrace. Her pulse jumped, and her body shivered. "April," he murmured, "this is important to both of us."

Of course, this was the deal they'd made. "Right."

She put her arms around his neck and fell into the role of fiancée, kissing him back, kissing him as if he was her whole world. Let them take all the pictures they needed to. This charade would be over soon and she'd be able to go on with her life.

Risk made a good show of it, kissing her longer than she expected, and when he finally broke off the kiss, he was as breathless as she was. They'd always had chemistry, and she wouldn't give it any real credence that his eyes nearly smoked like hot coals. It was all for show.

"I think we've convinced them," she whispered, her lips tingling.

"Yep," he said, his gaze roaming over her face. "Good job."

Good job? She'd laid her best kisses on him.

It had been an extraordinary job, at the very least.

Eight

The next day April and Jenna drove down the highway heading back from Willow Springs, a sapphire-blue ball gown hanging in a garment bag from a hook in the back seat. "Jenna, I can't thank you enough for taking the morning off from the salon to shop with me."

"You're welcome. You're going to look great at the big Founder's Day dinner."

"Thank you. How about we go to lunch? My treat this time. Where do you want to go? I'll take you anywhere *except* the Farmhouse Grill."

Jenna's eyes rounded, her mouth dropped open and as their eyes met, both of them burst out laughing. "Okay, how about Italian then?"

"Sounds delish."

A short time later, they entered Italia Ristorante,

and April immediately wanted to make a dash for it. "Oh man. Do you see what I see?"

Shannon was sitting with Risk in a corner booth with a handful of reporters and cameramen hovering nearby. She was all in black, from the bomber jacket and sequined top to her jeans and knee-high boots. Her ruby-red lips matched her fingernails, and the whole package screamed *well put together*. April would look silly in clothes like that, but on Shannon, it worked.

She'd had no idea Risk was having lunch here, apparently with Shannon.

"Is it too late to run?" Jenna asked.

"I'm afraid so…we've been spotted."

A cameraman rushed over and snapped their picture, and a reporter stuck a microphone close to her face. "Are you here to have lunch with Shannon and your fiancé? Did you know he was dining with Shannon Wilkes today?"

Risk glanced her way, and she caught his quick frown before he transformed it into a charming smile. He rose from his seat and made his way over. "Sweetheart," he said, brushing his lips over hers as he wrapped his arm around her waist. Her ears burned from all the attention, and the kiss to ward off the suspicious press simply pissed her off. "It's so good to see you," he said. "Hello, Jenna."

"Hello," Jenna answered.

Risk made sure to keep his attention on April, his dark eyes soft on her. He'd had practice being the focus of attention. She wasn't as smooth or polished, and a gnawing ache began to grow in her belly. She'd seen the look on Shannon's face when she had Risk all to herself, well…all to herself and her adoring press.

"I ran into Shannon here today, and she sat down and joined me for a few minutes while I wait for my meeting with the mayor," he explained as photos were being snapped.

"Were you checking up on your fiancé, Miss Adams?" a reporter asked.

She smiled at the reporter, then gave Risk an adoring look. "Risk and I happen to love this restaurant and each other. My friend and I came by to pick up something to eat. It's an added bonus that I get to see him for a few minutes during the day."

By now, all eyes in the restaurant were on them. She couldn't blame anyone. It was a juicy story—Risk appearing to be caught with his ex by his present fiancée.

Optics were important. She was sure the headlines in the morning would inflame more than flatter.

Antonio, the owner of the restaurant, came over and apologized for the disturbance. Then he tactfully told the paparazzi they were bothering his customers and they would be effectively tossed out if they didn't leave quietly.

Shannon sauntered over, standing directly beside Risk, close enough to rub shoulders. To his credit he moved slightly away, but Shannon wasn't to be ignored. "Hello again, April."

"Hello, Shannon. I'd like you to meet my dear friend Jenna. Jenna, this is Shannon Wilkes."

The women nodded in greeting.

"I hope you don't mind me sitting with Risk for a

while. We bumped into each other quite by accident."
She smiled, her eyes lighting on Risk. "We were kill-
ing time, reminiscing. Lord knows, we have stories
that could fill up a whole book. Don't we, Risk?" She
gave him a classic Shannon Wilkes smile.

"We were talking about Shannon's mom," he explained. "She was a great baker."

"They say the way to a man's heart is through his
stomach. And Mom always made Risk his favorite
desserts."

"You mean she baked caramel peach pie?" April
asked.

"Why, yes, she did. And butter cookies with—"

"Fresh-crushed walnuts on top."

Shannon's smug expression faltered a bit. "Yes, yes,
that's right."

Risk darted his gaze April's way, their eyes meeting
ever so briefly, before he granted Shannon a smile. Apparently their life-story-in-an-hour training session had
paid off. "I always appreciated Mary's baking for me."

"She loved you very much," Shannon said softly.

"She was a special lady."

Risk's phone buzzed. "Sorry, I have to take this. It's
from Mayor Addison," he said, stepping away from
the three of them.

Shannon eyed April. "Do you have any news for
me about the house?" Her voice was sugary sweet, yet
calculation entered her sage eyes.

"Oh, uh, yes, I do. That's one of the things I was
going to do this afternoon, call you. I'm afraid the
Russo family isn't interested in your offer."

Shannon's gaze moved to where Risk was standing in the back of the restaurant, speaking into his phone. "Offer them twenty thousand more."

April gulped, and Jenna stared at Shannon like she'd lost her mind. The original offer, along with this added bonus, was outrageously generous. Shannon really wanted this place. "I can certainly do that, but why, uh, does it have to be that particular farmhouse? I have several listings that are equally as nice."

Shannon's eyes sparkled as a faraway expression stole over her face. "It's personal."

She got it. It was personal between her and Risk.

"I'll see what I can do."

Risk returned to join them, looking none too happy. "The mayor had to cancel our meeting. How about I take all three of you out to lunch today?"

"I'm in," Shannon announced immediately.

Risk gave April a pointed look, as if he'd strangle her if she refused.

"You know what? I have to get back to the salon, so thanks anyway," Jenna said. "But don't hesitate to stay, April. Have a good lunch, everyone!"

Jenna, the rat, abandoned her. Some friend she turned out to be. Weren't besties supposed to stick together? Now, she was stuck having lunch with Risk and his very flirty, very flamboyant ex-love, Shannon Wilkes.

The next night Risk stood outside April's apartment door. She wasn't going to like this, but he had no choice, so he knocked hard and hoped she would answer. It'd be easier to explain in person why he had to add to their list of appearances. He'd argue his case face-to-face rather than try to reason with her over the phone. He'd tried calling her today, and they'd gotten disconnected. Or she'd hung up on him. He wasn't sure which.

He knocked a second time and heard her call out, "Who is it?"

"It's Risk. I need to speak with you."

"What are you doing here?"

"Let me in and I'll explain."

"Hold on a sec. I just got out of the tub."

Visions of her naked body, all wet and round and beautiful, filled his head. She had curves in all the right places, and all too often lately he caught himself thinking about the two nights of mind-blowing sex he'd had with her. He wished he didn't remember. He wasn't as immune to her as he let on. Pretending to be her fiancé meant caresses and kisses that weren't all that benign, that stirred his blood and racked his body.

He wasn't forgetting her lies or how she'd made a fool out of him. That was the one thing keeping him in check.

The door opened, and there she stood, wearing some sort of silky kimono robe wrapped tightly at her waist. Her hair was up in a messy bun, and her face was washed clean of makeup. Makeup she didn't need, not with those big blue eyes and rosy lips. The subtle scent of fresh flowers immediately perfumed the air around her. They stared at each other a moment.

"Risk? Why are you here?" she asked.

"Please let me in. It'll look weird if you don't." He played the fake fiancée card and slid a glance around the building grounds, pretty darn sure he hadn't been followed tonight.

She opened the door wider, making room for him to come in, a frown on her face. Okay, maybe he should've called first and warned her he'd be coming over. But that meant risking she wouldn't hear him out.

The moment he stepped inside, he immediately noticed the starkness of the place. Things seemed different than the first time he'd been here. All the touches that made this apartment warm and homey seemed to be gone.

"Where were you today when we got disconnected?" he asked, trying to sound casual.

She sighed. "At the lodge."

"I tried you several times. Couldn't get through."

"I've been overseeing some work. The cell service out there is temperamental."

He nodded and glanced around again. "Why does this place look so different?"

"Let's just say I've been doing some…spring-cleaning."

"In the winter?"

"Well, it'll be spring in a few months." She folded her arms across her middle. "Risk, I'm tired. I've had a busy day. What do you need from me?"

"Why don't we sit down? You look like you could use a drink…to relax. How about we open a bottle of wine?" Her lips parted in feigned outrage, and he grinned. April was getting to be a pretty good actress, but tonight he wasn't buying it. His suggestion brought temptation to her eyes.

"Why don't you tell me why you want to ply me with alcohol?"

"You mean, aside from the obvious reason?"

"Which is?"

"You look hot in that getup."

She grabbed her robe at the lapels and pulled it tighter around her, her face flaming a bit. "This from the guy who can't stand me."

"I never said that." Well, not those exact words, but he had reamed her out pretty badly when he'd gotten his memory back. Still, he had blood in his veins, and it surprised him how attracted he was to her, even after all she'd done. "You're a beautiful woman, April," he said quietly. "It'd be hard not to notice."

She slumped onto the sofa, and he took a seat at the opposite end.

"Why are you buttering me up?" Suspicion darkened her eyes.

He chose not to answer.

"Speak."

He laughed. "You know, you're a worthy contender, April."

"I'll take that as a compliment. Go on."

He sighed, ready for the stuffing to hit the fan. "Okay, I know we agreed on an agenda, but some things have come up recently, and we need to make adjustments. Believe me, I wouldn't ask if it wasn't important. You see, since the mayor had to cancel our appointment, he called to invite both of us to dinner at his home tomorrow night. His wife would like to meet you. Apparently she went to school with your mother."

"No."

"April, be reasonable."

"I'm not going to dinner at the mayor's house and pretending…pretending we're in love. That's too intimate a setting for me. Sorry. Just tell him I've got the flu, was bitten by a rabid dog, broke my ankle. I don't care what excuse you make. I'm behind on my work, and I can only take so much at a time."

He rubbed the back of his neck and sighed. "All right, that was a long shot," he said, giving in. "I'll make an excuse for you. *None* of the ones you suggested, but I'll come up with something."

"Good." Her nod brought his gaze up to her messy bun, bopping up and down. He liked her look tonight: cute and sexy. Even though she had a perpetual frown on her face, or maybe because of it, he was drawn to her. "But this next item on the agenda I hope you'll consider. It's for our aunt Lottie. With Founder's Day coming up in just five days, she probably thinks we've forgotten her sixty-second birthday. She's rarely at Rising Springs on her birthday, so Drea had this idea to give her a surprise party day after tomorrow. It's family and a few close friends. Naturally, you should attend."

"But I barely know her."

"She's a good woman, April. And to the world, you're my fiancée."

"I know she's a good woman. She's treated me like family, which I find very sweet."

"I really think she'd like you to join us. You'll be with my family mostly, so very little pretending."

"That's a plus," she said all too quickly. "Will Shannon be attending?"

"Shannon?" That question came out of left field. "No, she's not invited. Why?"

April gave her shoulder a shrug. "Sometimes I think she's onto us. Whenever I see her or talk to her over the phone, she seems to be…testing me."

"How so?"

"Well, for instance she's been interested in buying the Russo property, and today I had to call her about it. Somehow she always finds a way to bring the subject back to you. She asks pointed questions and, well, it makes me uncomfortable. And then there's photos of us—you and me, or Shannon and me, or you and Shannon—plastered all over the news. It's a bit much."

"Did you say the Russo property?" *Holy crap.* Risk almost came out of his seat. What was Shannon up to? "That farmhouse on the edge of town?"

"Yes, she said she has personal reasons for wanting the place. And I think it has to do with you."

He had history with Shannon on that piece of property. Before it sold to the Russos, it had been a rental property, and Shannon had stayed there on her first visit to his hometown. The first time they'd made love in Boone Springs, it had been there. "You'd be right, April."

That's all he was going to say on the matter. They'd been so hot and heavy in those days, Shannon thought it best to stay somewhere off the ranch so they could have privacy day and night. Those days had been memorable, but now things were different.

"I see."

"I'm not restarting anything with Shannon." He had to make that clear to April, since they were in this together.

"You two looked pretty cozy sitting at the restaurant the other day."

"That was innocent. She walked in and spotted me at the table and came over to say hello. There was nothing illicit about it. It wasn't planned."

"There's been love triangle speculation all over the internet. This isn't easy for me."

"I get that, but that's why you should come to my aunt's birthday celebration. To dismiss the rumors. The more we look like a real engaged couple, the less speculation there'll be."

"Do you agree to see the lodge the very next day? It'll be ready to be viewed by then."

"The lodge?" He'd barely given it a thought. He'd been focused on keeping up his pretend-fiancé role and dealing with Founder's Day.

"Risk, you do remember our deal, don't you?"

He had to admire her gumption. She was a go-getter. "If I say yes, then you'll come to the celebration?"

She thought about it, making him sweat for a few lingering moments, and then her smile turned her eyes a soft baby blue and wiped the perpetual frown off her face.

"Yes," she said finally, "I'll come."

* * *

Late the next afternoon, after a full day of over-seeing the workmen at the lodge and putting her final touches on staging the rooms, April sat down at a café table at Katie's Kupcakes three blocks from her office. She and Katie had both grown up in Boone Springs, and today they'd shared a few cordial words before she'd ordered a decadent brownie cupcake with a vanilla almond latte. She was exhausted, so feeling guilty about her indulgence wasn't even a remote consideration.

She'd worked her butt off this week, and she deserved a treat.

She sipped her delicious drink and then bit into her cupcake. "Oh wow," she groaned. Two bites later, she spotted Lottie Brown walking into the bakery. She had a smile on her face and looked well put together in a rose-colored blouse tucked into a belted denim skirt with pretty studded boots to finish off the look. Lottie had style and grace. April liked how she didn't let her age bring polyester into her life.

Lottie spotted her immediately and walked over. "Hi, April." She glanced at her partially eaten cupcake. "Seems like you and I had similar cravings today."

"Did we?"

"I'm here for Katie's chocolate explosion cupcake."

"Would you care to join me?" April's manners had her asking, but she wasn't entirely sure that was all it was. Lottie was someone she wouldn't mind getting to know better.

"I'd love to." Lottie took a seat, and within a minute Katie came over to take her order.

"Katie, it's good to see you. You haven't been out to the ranch in a while."

"No, I've been busy. You know, with the bakery and my work at the horse rescue, I hardly know what day it is anymore."

"Mason and Drea's wedding is coming up, too."

"I'm looking forward to it. I've got to get my act together and plan Drea's bachelorette party, too."

"I'm sure you'll do a great job," Lottie said.

"I hope so. This is my first time…as maid of honor," she said, then bit her lip.

April knew something about Katie's strained relationship with the Boones. Five years ago, Lucas had broken off his engagement to Katie's sister right before the wedding. Katie was to be Shelly's maid of honor. Her sister had been stunned and devastated, which put Katie in a tough spot. She and Lucas had been friends. Not so much anymore.

Katie took Lottie's order and walked off. Lottie turned to her. "April, it's good to see you. Tell me, how's my nephew treating you?"

It was such an unexpected question, she paused a second. "Risk? Oh, just f-fine."

"Glad to hear it. You two are both good people. I wouldn't want either of you being hurt again."

"That's very kind of you to say. I'm sure…we'll part ways without any fireworks."

Lottie raised her brows and then changed the subject, much to April's relief. As they conversed, April found she had a good deal in common with Lottie, from the kind of music and books they liked to their sense of style and design.

Half an hour later, April walked out of the bakery with Lottie. "I'm glad we bumped into each other," April said.

"Me, too." Lottie sighed and stared into her eyes. "If I can say something… I sorta wish you and my nephew were the real thing. I see you together, and it just feels right. I hate to say it, but I knew going in that Risk and Shannon weren't going to work. But I'm just Risk's favorite aunt. What do I know?" She rolled her eyes, as if mocking herself.

April laughed, not at all insulted by Lottie's earnest opinion. Of course, she didn't agree with her. She and Risk would never work. "Sorry to disappoint you, but I don't think we'll—"

"Oh no! Would you look at that!"

Lottie took off running, following a blond sheepdog trotting into the middle of the street. "Here, boy, here, boy," she called out, trying to coax him to safety. But the dog kept moving. "Get out of the street! Go, go."

Lottie didn't see the car rounding the corner. "Lottie!"

April ran as fast as her legs would carry her. She heard the screech of tires, saw the car swerving right before she shoved Lottie out of the way. April went down, her knees scraping the blacktop as she fell, the smell of burning rubber reaching her nostrils, the heat of the car's engine blasting in her face.

She opened her eyes and stared at the big blue sky,

and then Lottie appeared in her line of vision. "Dear Lord, April. Are you okay? Did you hit your head?"

"No, no. I'm fine. I think." She did a mental scan of her body. She hadn't hit her head when she went down. And she hadn't been hit; she fell while pushing Lottie out of the way of the car. It was a stumble and luckily only her knees were bruised under her skirt, though she was pretty sure her whole body would be sore as hell tomorrow, because that's how it worked. Fall today, ache tomorrow.

"You saved me and put yourself in danger. You could have been hit by that car," Lottie said. "That was a very brave thing to do. Thank you. I don't know what to say." Tears welled up, and she wiped them away. "Do you think you can get up?"

"I think so."

Lottie took hold of April's hands and helped her up. She straightened, locking her bruised knees, her entire body shaking. She felt her knees burn now as a small amount of blood oozed out. "We should get you to a doctor," Lottie said.

By then, a crowd had formed, and the lanky young driver of the vehicle came over, a look of fright on his teenage face. The car had come to a careening halt only inches from where April had fallen. "I'm so sorry," he said. "I didn't see anyone when I made the turn."

"It's not your fault, young man," Lottie said. "I chased after a dog darting out into the street, and you did your best to avoid hitting anyone. If anything, you did a great job," Lottie assured him.

He nodded. "Miss, are you gonna be okay?" he asked April.

"Yes, I think I'll be fine. I'm just shaken up a bit."

"Should I call nine-one-one?" a voice from the small crowd asked.

"Oh no, please. I'm going to be fine." April looked out into the sea of people gathering.

Cell phones were pointed her way as onlookers snapped pictures of her. She heard whispers. Some had recognized her as Risk Boone's fiancée.

"Let me take you to the doctor, at least," Lottie said gently, taking her by the arm and leading her to the sidewalk in front of Katie's Kupcakes.

"Lottie, I think I'll go home and clean up my bruises. It's nothing serious."

Katie ran over, handing her a washcloth. "Here you go. It's clean. I rinsed it with cold water. If you'd like to come inside the bakery, you can clean up in there, April."

"That's a good idea," Lottie said.

"No, that's not necessary, Katie. But thank you for the washcloth." The last thing she wanted to do was make a scene. Once news got out, which was sure to happen with all the photos that were being snapped, reporters would show up. Her body cried out for rest. It had been a busy, crazy day. She dabbed at her knees with the cloth. They were only bleeding slightly, and the washcloth really helped. "That feels better."

"Let me drive you home. I insist," Lottie said.

Lottie wanted to help, and April wouldn't deprive her. "Okay, thanks."

She walked arm in arm with Lottie Brown to her car parked a short distance down the street. Once April put on her seat belt, Lottie turned to her, her usually jovial face sober and concerned. "Are you sure you don't need a doctor?"

"I'm sure."

"How about I take you to Rising Springs, where we can take care of your bruises and let you rest."

"I wouldn't think of it, Lottie."

"You are Risk's fiancée."

"For the rest of the week only." After their conversation about Risk being right for her, April had to remind Lottie their engagement had a very short shelf life. She and Risk had no future.

Lottie pursed her lips, admitting defeat. "Okay, to your apartment then. Point the way."

April gave her directions, and Lottie drove carefully, going ever so slowly. That's when April realized Lottie had been shaken up, too. As Lottie parked in front of April's apartment complex, she asked, "Lottie, I didn't hurt you with that shove, did I?"

"Considering I might've been flattened like a pancake if you hadn't come to my rescue, I'm doing great. Don't even think about it." Lottie took April's hand and gave it a squeeze. "I can't thank you enough." Then Lottie reached over and gave April a big, squishy, loving, mama bear hug.

She relished the feel of the older woman's arms around her. She hadn't been hugged like this in a long time, and it made her miss her own mother, who was in Spain at the moment. Lottie lent her comfort and showed her gratitude, which was what she needed right now. Once the embrace ended, April smiled at the older woman. "Thanks for the ride."

"Can I walk you to your door?"

"That's sweet, but not necessary. I'll be fine. I just need to rest."

"Okay then. Be sure to call if you need anything."

"I promise I will. Goodbye, Lottie."

April got out of the car, her knees still burning, but she waved to Lottie and watched her drive off before she turned to enter her apartment complex. She really needed to cleanse her wounds and collapse on her bed.

"April!"

Hearing the fast pace of footsteps behind her, she squeezed her eyes shut.

Oh no.

It was Risk.

Nine

"April," Risk called again.

What was he doing here? He was supposed to be having dinner with the mayor. She stopped walking and turned, bumping into his chest. He'd been right behind her. "Oh."

He reached for her, holding her arms still. "I heard what happened," he said softly.

"Already?" She knew what they said about small towns, but this was crazy.

"Katie called me. I was in town, at the office. Are you okay?"

Genuine concern entered his eyes as he scanned her body up and down. "You're bleeding."

She looked down. A few tiny droplets of blood trailed down her legs.

Before she could react, Risk scooped her up in his arms and began carrying her to her apartment. She clung to his neck, a bit shocked by his bold move. And a little bit turned on. It was a white-knight sort of thing for a man to do, one that many women secretly fantasized about. "I can walk, Risk. You don't need to carry me."

"Yes, I do. You were limping."

"I was not limping."

"I say you were."

"That's because you—" Then it hit her, and she lowered her voice. "Oh, I get it. You think someone's watching us, taking pictures."

He snapped his eyes to hers, his face twisting into a scowl. "Yep, you got it. That's why I'm carrying you."

She clamped her mouth shut, uneasy at the tone of Risk's voice, the look on his face. Something was off, and suddenly she wasn't sure about anything. Maybe it was fatigue, but being in Risk's arms again, soaking up his strength, breathing in his musky scent didn't feel all so terrible.

"Give me your key," he said as they reached her front door. She snatched her key from her purse and he unlocked the door.

"You don't need to baby me," she said softly, noticing his jaw twitch.

"Don't I?" He brought her into the apartment and laid her down on the sofa. "Stay still, April. Don't move. I'm gonna take care of your knees."

"Risk, you don't…"

But he was already walking down her hallway. She

heard him scavenging around her bathroom, and after a few moments he was back with a handful of medical supplies, a look of determination on his face.

He sat at the foot of the sofa and gently pushed up the hem of her dress. His fingers brushing her thighs sent hot waves zipping up and down her legs.

"Let me know if it hurts," he said, fully intent on his task. He began applying a soapy cloth to her knees and the thin trail of blood running down her legs. He wiped her knees dry and lathered the wounds with antibiotic cream. "What you did today," he began, then cleared his throat, "was a foolish thing."

Her eyes flashed to his.

"You could've been killed."

He sounded sincere. "I didn't think so. I just reacted, calculating I could get to Lottie before the car mowed her down."

Risk bandaged both knees. It wasn't a pretty sight, but she did feel better not having open wounds. "You saved my aunt's life, April."

"Maybe."

"Not maybe. I saw the video."

"There's a video? My God." How on earth did that happen so quickly?

"It's the world we live in today. Someone on the scene sent it to the *Tribune*, and they immediately called for my reaction."

"And you rushed right over here?"

He nodded.

"What about your dinner with the mayor and his wife?"

"What better reason to cancel than my fiancée getting injured in an accident? He wouldn't expect any less from me."

"Because it wouldn't look right." Of course. That had to be it. "Sorry, I know that dinner was important to you."

"It's just business, April. It's not as important as—"

"I'm surprised you didn't want to see your aunt," she interrupted, stopping Risk from saying anything she didn't want to hear. She couldn't start believing he actually cared about her, actually worried about her well-being.

"Katie assured me Aunt Lottie is fine. I'll talk to her in a little while."

"Well, thank you for patching me up. My mom would say we're even Steven."

"How so?"

"I took care of you when you lost your memory, and you just repaid the favor."

He ran his hand down his face, staring at her for a moment. "April."

"You really don't have to stay. I'm fine now." And he'd done his fake-fiancé duty by rushing over here to check on her.

He set his jaw, stubbornly. She'd seen that determined look before. "You must be thirsty," he said, ignoring her comment. "Let me get you some water."

"Water? A glass of wine would be more like it," she blurted. As long as he was going to stay, she might as well have a real drink. She deserved one after the day she'd had.

"Got it." He rose, and she watched him make his way into her kitchen. She heard cabinets being opened and glasses clinking. He popped his head out of the doorway. "Red or white?"

"Red, please."

He smiled, a killer smile giving her silly nerves a workout. There was something different about him tonight. He was being...nice.

Because he felt he owed her something for saving Lottie.

By the time he returned with two goblets of wine, April was sitting up. He handed her a glass. "Thank you." He sat and met her eyes again. "You tired?"

"I was. It's been a crazy day, but now I think I'm a bit too antsy to sleep."

"There's a great movie on right now."

"Which one?"

"A Day in the Life."

It was one of her top-ten favorites. They'd discussed this just a few days ago. "A girlie movie. I'm up for that."

"Me, too."

The wineglass halted midway to her lips. "You're going to watch it, too?"

He shrugged. "For a little while, until I finish my wine. If that's okay?"

"Oh, um. Yeah, for a little while. You'll be in charge of the remote."

Risk already had it in his hand. He turned on the TV and began channel surfing. "Ah, here it is."

April relaxed into the cushions of the sofa, the wine

taking the edge off. She eyed Risk, who was also set-tling in. He appeared at ease. They'd never done this before…just be. Like a regular couple.

She couldn't stop the warm exciting thrill traveling the length of her body.

Was it the wine? Or was it Risk?

Whatever it was, she liked the way she was feel-ing right now.

The next afternoon April and Clovie had just fin-ished a quick lunch at the diner and were walking the two short blocks back to the office when Clovie nudged her arm. "Don't look across the street," she said qui-etly. "And keep walking, unless you want to be pho-tographed again."

April put her head down and did as her friend said. "Why, what's happening?"

"Looks like Shannon and…uh, your fiancé are to-gether outside the bank. Shannon's speaking to a bunch of reporters swarming them."

April slid a glance that way and saw for herself. She had no idea what was going on. Risk was like a mag-net to the woman. She seemed to seek him out, finding ways to insinuate herself into his life. It hadn't both-ered April before, and it shouldn't bother her now, but Risk had been so kind to her last night. She didn't re-member him leaving, but she'd woken up on her sofa around midnight, tucked cozily into the one blanket throw she hadn't brought to the lodge. The TV was off, the door was locked. And this morning, she'd found his note.

Hope you slept tight.
Take care of those pretty knees—
we have dancing to do.
I'll pick you up at 6 p.m.
Risk

The note was a welcome sight and had put her in a good mood this morning despite being sore and achy. She'd almost called Risk to thank him for taking care of her. But he was with Shannon now, out in public, and April wanted no part of it. She had enough going on in her life. She'd been asked to do a local radio show, a segment on her heroism saving Lottie Brown, which she politely turned down. And there were photos of the whole thing and articles written on the internet and in the *Tribune*.

The only positive coming out of this was that the Adams Agency was getting a load of good publicity, and that never hurt. But she wasn't sure if that one positive could overcome all the negatives.

Their engagement was a big fat fraud.

And her fake fiancé was busy spending the afternoon with his ex-girlfriend.

Risk straightened his collar and brushed lint from his stitched dark gray sports jacket as he stood outside April's door, ready to knock. After dealing with Shannon for most of the afternoon, he was looking forward to a night out with April. He wouldn't say his fake fiancée was low maintenance after all the trouble she'd caused, but she sure as hell was a lot easier to deal with than his superstar ex.

He knocked, and it took her a while to answer the door. But when she did, it was well worth the wait. "Wow." He liked her in red, and this dress fit her to a tee, accentuating the curves he found so damn appealing. Her hair was down, the curly tendrils framing her face. "You look gorgeous, April."

"Thank you," she said. "It's not too much? I have no idea where we're going, but your note mentioned dancing?"

He took his hat off and ran his hand through his hair. "You got my note. Good. Yes, dancing if you're up to it. The family rented out Aunt Lottie's favorite restaurant for the evening—not one our family owns, for a change. The Garden House."

"I've heard about it. All good things." April opened the door wider and let him inside the apartment. She went about picking up a black clutch and sweater from the sofa arm.

"How are your knees?" Her dress was covering them, which he assumed was a deliberate move on her part.

She frowned. "They're not pretty."

"Let me take a look."

She flinched, her eyes opening wide.

"I have a vested interest, since I was your Florence Nightingale last night."

"Not by choice."

She tested him time and again, and he could easily lose patience, but he held himself in check. "April, please."

She gave him a look as if to say this was above his pay grade as her fake fiancée, but he didn't care. His uncanny concern sort of baffled him, too, but he was determined to see how she was healing. They stared at each other a few seconds, and finally she shrugged.

"Oh, okay. It was nice of you to help me last night," she admitted, though it sounded like she had to force the words out of her mouth. She lifted the hem of her dress a few inches and showed him her injuries.

To gain a better view, he bent and cupped the back of her right leg, which was a big mistake. She was soft there and firm all at the same time. Touching her flesh sent a pang of desire shooting down to his groin. It was instantaneous, and crazy. She'd been on his mind lately. He couldn't help wondering if he'd misjudged her. Wondering if she'd been caught up in something bigger than the both of them. He glimpsed her left knee and then took a hard swallow. "They, uh, they look much better."

"You think so?"

He rose and met her gaze, taking in the warm blue glow in her eyes. "Yeah...you're healing fine."

"Thanks, Dr. Boone."

They both chuckled, easing the tension in the room, but then her gaze landed on him again and she laid one hand on his chest, to keep him near or to keep her distance—he wasn't sure. Whatever it was, heat rushed to his chest where her palm rested. "Risk, I saw you today…with Shannon. I suppose I'll read all about it in tomorrow's newspaper."

Risk looked away, mentally cursing. He'd been the one harping on April to keep up this pretend engagement while Shannon seemed intent on derailing it. "It isn't what you think."

"I don't know what to think, but you're the one who needs the world to believe we're engaged. And you keep showing up with your ex. It puts me in a bad position."

"I know, I know." He blew out a breath and shook his head. "Shannon wanted to make a sizable donation to the Boone Foundation. It's a charity my parents started when Mason was born, and all proceeds go to underprivileged children in Boone County. She asked me to meet her at the bank, and as we were walking out together, reporters were there for the story, most likely summoned by her. I should've expected it, since this was always Shannon's MO. Doing a good thing is a trade-off for the positive publicity she gets."

"Is that all it was?"

"That and lunch at the Farmhouse."

April blinked. "You had lunch with her again? After all the warnings you've given me about being careful. I'm sorry, Risk, but that wasn't—"

"You're not jealous, are you?" Risk's chest swelled at the thought of her being jealous, and that confused the hell out of him. Both Shannon and April had played him. So why in hell was he humming inside? And looking at April differently tonight?

"I am not jealous," she said defiantly, her face turning a shade of pink, "so let the air out of that balloon, Risk."

He smiled. She *was* jealous.

"I'm…concerned. But if you don't mind blowing your cover, then it's on you. I'm holding up my end of the bargain."

"Right, okay. Got it. Are you ready? We can't be late for Aunt Lottie's surprise party."

"I'm as ready as I'll ever be." She rolled her eyes adorably, and Risk had to rein in his emotions. He was starting to like April Adams again. He couldn't seem to help it.

She headed for the front door. "Let the show begin."

Risk only smiled at that and took her hand as he led her to his car.

Risk didn't think the surprise party for Aunt Lottie could go any smoother. Her dear friend Wanda, who lived in Willow County, had brought her to the Garden House, and as soon as she'd walked into the restaurant, the roomful of twenty-five of Aunt Lottie's good friends and family members shouted, "Surprise!"

Aunt Lottie jerked back, tears welling in her eyes as she looked around at all the people who mattered in her life. She seemed genuinely surprised. "I wasn't expecting this," she declared to everyone.

"Tell me you didn't think we'd forget your birthday?" Drea stepped up and hugged Lottie. "This time, we wanted to surprise you."

"Well, you certainly did."

Mason put his arm around Aunt Lottie's shoulder

and kissed her cheek. "My fiancée gets all the credit for this. You know she's an expert at planning parties."

"Drea is the best," Lottie said, love entering her eyes. "And this place is just right. Thank you all for coming."

Mason and Drea looked good together. Risk's older brother was totally in love, and he'd never been happier in his life.

Risk glanced at April standing beside him, and a sharp pang hit him in the gut. He'd vowed not to get involved with her again, and he was trying to stick to that, but it was getting harder these days. After her deception, at first they hadn't liked each other, but that was hardly true anymore. He was beginning to like her too much, not only because she'd sacrificed herself for his aunt's safety, but because she was hardworking, dedicated, *sweet*.

Sweet? Oh man, he wanted April.

Their eyes met now, hers brilliant blue and sparkling with life. He liked her curly hair bounding past her shoulders, her lush ruby-red lips matching the hot dress she wore.

April was no longer persona non grata in his family. She was a superhero, and that worked on his conscience. He'd called her a lot of horrible things in the past, hated how she'd played him for a fool, but he hadn't exactly been perfect, either. The first time they'd been together, he'd walked out on her, and she'd deserved more than that.

She smiled at him, and his heart did a little flip.

Somehow, he didn't think it was a phony smile meant to please onlookers. This smile was real, meant for him.

He took her hand and smiled back at her, then led her over to Aunt Lottie and kissed the older woman's cheek. "Happy birthday. What are you, thirty-nine again?"

Lottie placed her palm on the side of his face. "I'll never tell. And neither will you, if you know what's good for you."

The three of them laughed. "This is such a wonderful surprise," she continued. "I thought I was having a quiet dinner with Wanda. And now, you and all my favorite people are here to help me celebrate." She turned toward April, taking her hand, her eyes soft and sincere. "I'm so touched that you're here, April. It means a lot to me."

"I wouldn't have missed it."

She nodded, glancing from April to him, a sweet smile on her face. "You both look wonderful tonight. A real handsome couple."

Then Lottie was whisked away by Drea and her father. Drew was being a bit of a sourpuss tonight. He seemed to be going through the motions for the family's sake but he'd been grumbling a lot about Lottie nearly getting herself killed running after that dog.

Those two always seemed at odds.

Formally dressed waiters came around with trays of appetizers. Risk and April took a few and walked around the restaurant. April was fascinated by the lush gardens groomed to perfection inside the dining rooms. Palms and greenery along with flowering plants and vertical gardens of ivy, moss and trailing vines made up the perimeter of the room. A five-piece band stood at the ready on a small stage in front of a dance floor.

"Hmm, this is so good," she said taking a bite out of a miniature beef Wellington. "The pastry is so light."

He'd already swallowed down two. "Sure is."

He liked that April enjoyed food and wasn't shy about it. He'd been on dates with women who'd eat nothing but salad. In Texas, that wasn't a meal—it was barely a side dish—and April seemed to feel that way, too. "Not as good as peanut butter and cranberry muffins, though."

She glanced at him. Uh-oh, was that also a memory she didn't want to rehash?

"No," she said, her voice breathless. "Nothing's better than our survival food."

"Yeah, about that. I've never thanked you for taking good care of me when I was injured."

"I know."

He'd been too angry when he'd found out about her lies that he'd ignored the care she'd given him. Care that he hadn't wanted to acknowledge until recently.

"I'm thanking you now, and I mean it, April." He spoke straight from his heart this time.

"I believe you do."

"Seems you've saved two members of my family this month."

"Is that why you're being nice to me?"

"It's not just that." He paused for a second and then

gave her the honest truth. "Maybe you're easy to be nice to."

"Maybe, huh?"

The lights dimmed, a spotlight finding the band as they started playing, and all Risk could think about was holding April in his arms. He put out his hand. "Dance with me?"

She looked around as others were heading to the dance floor, including Aunt Lottie with his brother Luke. "It'll make Aunt Lottie happy," he added.

"Well in that case, for the birthday girl," April said, taking his hand.

Fortunately, the band played a slow love song. As they reached the dance floor, Risk drew April into his arms, her sweet scent wafting to him. She moved fluidly with him, her body limber and easy to lead. They touched often, her breasts brushing his chest, and he had trouble staying focused on the music. His heart beat hard; his body was revved up. She laid her head on his shoulder, her silky blond locks teasing his nostrils.

"April," he whispered, lowering his hands onto the small of her back and drawing her closer. She was too much of a temptation for him, too close for his sanity. His instincts taking over now, he bent his head and claimed her lips in a soft kiss.

She opened her eyes and looked up at him. "Are there reporters here?"

"I don't think so."

"Is it for the others, then?"

He shook his head. "What others? I only see you."

She smiled and so did he, and then he pressed his lips to hers again.

After the song ended, he pulled back to gaze into her eyes. The dewy, soft way she was looking at him stirred him up inside.

Luke walked up to them, interrupting their moment. "Mind if I cut in, Risker?"

Hell, yeah, he minded. His brother had to choose this moment to break in? It was bad timing, but it was also Aunt Lottie's night and he wasn't going to cause a scene, though he hated letting April go. He gave his brother a warning look and then relented. "Sure enough, Luke boy."

Luke grinned at that. "We'll never live down our nicknames," he said to April.

"I think they're great. Does Mason have one?" she asked Luke.

"Nah, he wouldn't have it. If we called him Masey, he'd get his drawers in a knot. He's just plain Mason."

"Got it."

The music began again and Luke took April into his arms, leaving Risk to walk off the dance floor. He took a place at the back of the room, watching April smile at Luke as he danced her around the parquet floor.

Mason walked up and stood beside Risk. "Here you go," he said, handing him a bourbon on the rocks. They stood quietly for a while, sipping the liquor, Risk's gaze focused on April.

"You know, you've got it bad," Mason said.

He sipped his drink. "Do I?"

"Man, Aunt Lottie nearly applauded when you kissed April right there on the dance floor."

"She likes April."

"So do you. A whole lot."

"Maybe."

"There's no maybes about it. You care for her. Either that or you ate some bad food, bro. You're turning green watching her with Luke."

His stomach squeezed tight. Was he ready for this? For opening up his heart again?

"Just saying, after this fake stuff is over, she's bound to move on. Maybe find another guy. Are you ready to face that?"

Picturing April with another man tied him up inside. "Is your sermon over?"

"Yep, all over. I think I got my point across."

Mason walked away smiling. He found Drea, the woman he was to marry soon, and gave her a giant kiss. Mason was in seventh heaven, totally committed to the woman he loved.

Risk had never been more envious of anyone in his life.

Her hand locked with Risk's, April walked dreamily to her apartment door. She'd had fun tonight, enjoying Lottie's birthday surprise and how the woman's face lit up as her loved ones gathered to celebrate her birthday. At the end of the evening, after a delicious dinner and dancing, Lottie had given a little speech, mentioning April's selflessness and heart, and had proposed a toast in her honor. Lottie had been sensitive enough not to put April in the spotlight, or drag out her thanks, but rather kept it light and cheerful.

Now, as the night came to an end, April was filled with a warm, wistful glow inside. "Thank you for a lovely evening," she said to Risk, laying her head against her door. "It was a beautiful night." Risk had been attentive, thoughtful, the perfect date.

"I'm glad." The huskiness in his voice, the deep penetrating look in his eyes, gave her heart a rattle. "I had a nice time, too," he said, running his index finger down her cheek. The slight touch sizzled on her skin and brought her gaze to his. "I liked holding you, dancing with you, kissing you," he whispered.

"You did?"

"Oh yeah." Then his hand was in her hair, playing with the curls.

She stared at his lips, firm and full and appealing. She set her palm on his jaw, loving the feel of his stubble under her fingertips. "Risk, this isn't for show, is it?"

He paused a second, thoughtful. "Feels pretty damn real to me." And then his mouth was on hers, taking away all doubt, all questions. He kissed her until she was breathless, her mouth ravaged, her body beginning to burn.

"Invite me in," he said between kisses.

"G-good idea."

As soon as the door was closed behind them, Risk pulled her sweater down her arms, taking it off and flinging it on the floor. Their lips melded together in another searing kiss. Breathing was hard, thinking impossible.

It was real this time. It felt right. "Bedroom," she murmured.

"Oh yeah." He whipped off his jacket and lifted her up, his arms strong and powerful underneath her as he carried her to the bed.

As he lowered her down, her feet hit the floor gently. Moonlight poured into the window, illuminating the hungry look in his eyes, the promise in his expression.

He touched her face, kissed her mouth and then whispered in her ear, "You're amazing, April."

Destiny seemed to keep bringing them together. The third time had to be the charm, because she certainly felt charmed tonight. She also felt a whole lot of things she didn't want to name.

Risk kissed her throat, trailing his lips farther down to nibble on her shoulders. His hands came around her back, and with sure, steady fingers he unzipped her dress. Cool air hit her for a second, until Risk's hands were on her again, warming her skin as he rubbed her back, his fingertips soothing her flesh.

She grabbed at his shirt and unbuttoned it, ready to get her hands on his granite chest. As she laid her palms there, raw heat seeped out, and a deep, appreciative groan rose from his throat.

"I love when you touch me," he whispered, right before his lips covered hers again.

"I love touching you," she whispered back.

Another groan escaped his throat, and then they were reaching for each other, removing clothes in a frenzy, his boots, her heels, his shirt, her dress. When April was down to her lacy black bra and panties, Risk stood back, admiring her. "You're perfect," he said, cupping her full breasts, kissing each one. Then he trailed his hands to the curve of her waist. "Just right here, too," he said, her skin heating under his palms. He caressed her hips, and her skin prickled under his touch. "These hips are sexy," he said. "Did you know that?"

She shook her head. She'd come to grips with her body and was no longer ashamed of her size, but no one had ever made her feel like this—like she was perfect and undeniably sexy—the way Risk was doing now.

He wrapped his hands around her hips to flatten his palms on her butt. Bringing her closer, he knelt down in front of her and removed her panties. Then he took her into his mouth, tightening his hold on her and using his tongue to make her wild. She whimpered as he stroked her over and over, the sensations hot and electric like tiny bolts of lightning. Out of her mind with pleasure, she clasped Risk's shoulders and hung on. And then she felt a pull, an internal magnet that took hold and wouldn't let go.

She moaned and Risk was there, keeping pace, bringing her higher and higher. When she finally broke apart, a shudder of pleasure racked her body. Trembling, she moaned and Risk rose then, bringing his mouth to hers, kissing her gently until her body calmed.

Then he lowered her onto her bed, took off his pants and joined her.

She wanted more of him, in the worst way. She brushed her mouth over his, relishing his firm lips, feeling his muscles tightening up, his body growing hard. There was a difference in him tonight, a look of fearless giving in his deep-set dark eyes she hadn't seen before. She wasn't imagining it—it *was* real this time.

And when their bodies merged, a sensual joining that made him close his eyes and grunt in pleasure, April gave him every bit of herself, leaving nothing back, kissing, caressing and loving him with a fierceness that came straight from her heart.

It was almost too powerful, too beautiful, too... much.

She came apart first, her body in glorious tatters once again. Her breaths came hard and fast and then Risk covered her mouth, kissed her again as he moved inside her. He held her arms above her head, covering her body, their skin pressed together, hot and sweaty.

"Oh man, sweetheart," he muttered through gritted teeth as he towered above her.

And found his way home.

April opened her eyes, her body easing into the morning. She felt languid and delicious waking up after an amazing night with Risk. She rolled over on her side, ready to cuddle, but he wasn't there. His warm rock-hard body she'd loved during the night was gone. She was hit with a momentary flash of déjà vu.

She rose from the bed, touching her feet to the floor, looking around for a note or some sign of him. All of his clothes were gone, too. Her joy immediately evaporated. That horrible feeling of abandonment seeped in again. She hated the feeling, hated thinking she wasn't worthy and feeling unlovable.

This wouldn't be the first time Risk had left her.

Damn you, Risk.

"Good mornin'. I see Sleeping Beauty has finally woken up." Risk strode into the bedroom, charming her with a smile. He walked right over to her and gave her a quick kiss on the lips. His appearance, that one kiss, woke her out of her misgivings. Risk was hardly a prince, but he was here. He hadn't deserted her again, and her relief overwhelmed her.

"Good morning back at ya."

Risk had showered; his hair was still damp and pushed away from his face. He smelled of her lavender soap and was wearing the clothes from last night.

"I, uh, guess I overslept."

"You deserved to. I kept you up late last night," he rasped.

"Yes, I remember." It would be hard to forget all the sensations she'd felt last night.

"April, you're good for me," he said, taking her into his arms. He held her tight, kissing the side of her cheek, gently rocking her back and forth.

God, she felt safe and cared for in his arms, and it worried her a bit. She still didn't fully trust him; if she did, she wouldn't have thought the worst this morning when she'd woken up to an empty bed.

"I hope you don't mind, I used your shower."

"Oh no. Not at all. Sorry I slept so late."

"I'm only glad you didn't wake up and think I ran out on you," he said.

When she didn't answer, he added, "Or did you?"

"I, uh, didn't have time to think. I was just getting up when you walked in." It was only partly a lie.

Risk gave her a nod.

"Well, if you still want to get an early start, we'd better get moving. I've got to stop by the office for a change of clothes."

Early start? Oh, right. She'd been so keyed into Risk, she almost forgot. "Yes, let me make us a quick breakfast, get dressed and then we'll drive out to the lodge."

"I've got breakfast covered," he said. "That's if you don't mind hard-boiled eggs, toast and juice?"

Her mouth dropped open. "You did all that?"

"It's hardly a culinary marvel, but yeah. I cooked."

She smiled. "Okay, then. Let's try out your meal, Chef Boone."

He took her hand and led her to the kitchen. But before they returned to the lodge, she had to get something off her chest first, something he'd accused her of doing that still ate away at her to this day.

She looked him square in the eye, determined to get her point across. "Just for the record, Risk, I'm asking you to keep what happened between us last night and your thoughts about the lodge separate. One has nothing to do with the other. Our deal was for you to give me your honest, objective opinion. That's all I'm asking."

Risk squeezed her hand. "I will. I promise."

She nodded. "Thank you. It matters to me that you know that. We both made mistakes, and hopefully we can put that behind us now."

"Yeah, I like the sound of that."

Ten

The lodge looked fabulous. The grounds were groomed, and a new coat of paint gave curb appeal a whole new meaning. April was proud of the mini renovations done to the property. But she wasn't the one who had to like it. Risk was. She gauged his reaction as he exited the car and opened the door for her.

He scanned the grounds with a thoughtful eye. "This place looks different in the daylight."

"It does," she agreed. "There's more to do out here, of course, but take a look around and see the potential. We can discuss anything you'd like."

She led him around back and showed him the view of Canyon Lake. It was a brisk but beautiful day, sunlight caressing the blue waters off in the distance. Just outside the dining area, café tables were set on the decking overlooking the lake, perfect for a morning breakfast and lunch, or a sunset dinner during the summer months.

"Canyon Lake is great for boating and fishing, and the area directly in front of us is designated for swimming. There's a slide that drops you ten feet out into the water. It's in bad shape but wouldn't cost much to replace," she said.

Risk was quiet, taking it all in. And then as they walked back around, he spent some time looking over the stables before he stopped at the woodshed and looked at the trees nearby. "One of those suckers nailed me," he said.

"I know. I never should've let you go get the wood."

"You had no choice," he said, puffing out his chest. "I wasn't going to let both of us freeze to death. Come on. Let's go inside."

April held her breath. She was super nervous about him seeing her vision for the place. As they entered the lobby area, Risk took a long look around, his gaze staying on the pieces she'd brought from her apartment. Furniture had been moved around. There were pictures on the walls.

"I see your influence here, April. You made the lodge homey, yet modern. Sort of like your own place."

"You noticed."

"Yeah. I never saw this place with sunlight streaming in."

"It's cheerful, isn't it? I had the wood beams conditioned."

Risk looked up and nodded. "Okay."

He walked around, testing the banister leading to the second story. He viewed the photos on the wall more closely and then gazed at the round rock fireplace that was the focal point of the room.

He made his way to the kitchen, and April's nerves squeezed tight. "We did some minor renovations here."

"You had the cabinets painted. They look good," he said. "And the appliances?"

"All in working order."

"The tiles are still chipped."

"The new owner can have his choice of new countertops."

He gave a quick nod. "What else do you have to show me?"

"The dining room and the master suite, down here. And then the upstairs."

She could tell Risk was impressed at how the dining room looked straight out onto Canyon Lake. The tables had vases full of flowers, and a few were set with dishes and cutlery. "You can almost see the guests dining here, enjoying the lake view."

Again, Risk only nodded.

When they walked into the master suite, Risk studied it thoroughly, glancing at the champagne and crystal flutes she'd had Clovie set on the dresser. It was too personal, too intimate, and she wished she hadn't taken that extra step when staging the room.

"Your vision," Risk whispered.

"It's just a suggestion on how…or rather… This is a special room," she said finally.

Risk looked at her and smiled. "I think so, too."

He took her hand and tugged her along. "Show me more."

They climbed the stairs. "How's the roof holding up?" he asked.

"We made minor repairs, but it will eventually need a new one. I can't do much about that."

As they reached the top of the stairs, she showed him each room, one by one, unable to keep the pride from her voice. "I really loved figuring out how to fix these rooms."

"You did this?" he asked.

"Well, I didn't physically paint them or remove pieces that didn't work. I gave the workmen those tasks. But I did make sure each room flowed, yet was unique as well. And I ordered all the new bedding."

"This is incredible, April."

"You really like it?"

He nodded. "You said you could transform the rooms, and you did it."

"Thank you." Her heart swelled from Risk's praise.

"Is there anything else you want to show me?"

"No, I think we've seen everything."

"So the business part of our day is over?"

"Y-yes, I suppose."

"Good, because I've been dying to do this all day." He tugged her into his arms, his hands wrapping smoothly around her waist as he lowered his mouth over hers and touched her lips. She felt his intensity even as he struggled to keep things tender and light. But with Risk, there didn't seem to be a middle ground.

He was too passionate a guy to hold back, and it was a big, big turn-on knowing he was so attracted to her.

She roped her arms around his neck and fell into the kiss. Parting her lips, she invited him in, and he swept through her mouth, causing heat to build and little sounds to emerge from deep in her throat. She could get lost in him and she warned herself to slow down, to not fall for him again. But she was scared silly it was too late.

When he ended the kiss first, both surprise and relief swamped her. He backed off, frowning as he glanced at his watch. "Shoot. We've got a long drive back to town, and I have an appointment at four today. If we don't stop now, we may never get out of here."

"You mean I would be stuck in here with you all day?" She batted her eyelashes.

"Yeah," he said, scrubbing his jaw and eyeing her. "On second thought, screw the appointment. Where were we?" He made a move toward her, and she immediately backed off.

"Not so fast, Romeo. I have work waiting for me, too."

"How about a late dinner then?"

"Sounds…perfect."

The next morning, April sat at her desk, going over the books quietly, disappointed she hadn't seen Risk last night. He'd sent her a text apologizing for his meeting going longer than he'd anticipated. The apology went a long way in making her feel better about her relationship with him, whatever that was.

Yet she was worried that Risk wasn't overly impressed with the lodge. She'd done all she could possibly do to make the place appealing. He'd been pretty quiet about it, praising her work but not really committing to the sale in any way. The little devil in her head thought he was stringing her along, but she refused to believe it.

Ten minutes later, she wasn't so sure of anything when Shannon Wilkes walked into the agency, a big satisfied grin on her face. "Hello, April. Hope it's okay that I'm here?"

April craned her neck to check outside the front window. "Did you bring your entourage?" Meaning, did she alert the press she was coming here?

"Gosh, I hope not. I have good news to share with you."

The best news would be she was leaving town. "What's that?"

"I went to see the Russos and made another offer on the house."

"You did what?" April wanted to jump out of her seat.

"I offered Tony Russo more money, and he said he couldn't afford *not* to take it. Anyway, looks like you and I are going to be neighbors."

"Shannon, you can't do that."

"Why not? It's not as if you had his listing or anything. He's agreed to sell me his house, and of course, I'll let you do the transaction. An easy commission for you."

"That's not how it's usually done."

"Yes, but we'll make it work, won't we?" Shannon flipped her long auburn hair to one side and gave her a sugary smile.

She had nerve. Barging into April's life like this, plotting to steal away her fiancé, fake as he was. "I'm gonna have to think about it, Shannon."

"Don't think too long. You need this sale. Last night when I spoke with Risk, he didn't sound like he was going to buy the lodge for the company. He made it seem—"

"You spoke with him last night?" When he was too busy to call her, too busy to have dinner with her? And he'd confided in Shannon about the lodge when he hadn't given April the courtesy of his answer.

"Yes, yes, I did. I'm in negotiations for a new project, and I needed Risk's advice."

"What does Risk know about making movies?" she asked casually while her stomach knotted up.

"Not much, but he knows me. He's the one who said I should slow down, take time for myself. He's been a good friend since my mama passed."

She could almost feel sorry for Shannon. Almost.

April glanced at her watch. "Shannon, I'm afraid I have an appointment with a potential client. Maybe we can speak about this later." Much later.

Shannon gave her a smug smile. "Of course. I'll be going. But please don't wait too long. I'm anxious to become Boone Springs' newest resident."

April forced a smile and watched the superstar leave, striding down the street like a princess.

While April felt anything but.

* * *

Ten minutes later, April stood at the reception desk at Boone Inc. "I'm April Adams. I'm here to see my fiancé, Risk Boone," she told the receptionist.

The woman came right to attention. "Of course, Miss Adams. Let me check if he's available." She picked up the phone.

"I'm available anytime for my fiancée," Risk said, striding out of a conference room. He had a big smile on his face. "April, sweetheart," he said, ready to kiss her. She gave him her cheek, and he eyed her before giving her a peck.

"Mr. Boone, I was just going to check if your meeting was over."

"Thanks, Dorothy. We just finished up and I spotted this beautiful lady waiting for me."

Again, he smiled at April, but she couldn't return the gesture. His brows furrowed, and he looked puzzled by her appearance here and her cold greeting. Good. She wasn't going to hide her head in the sand anymore. It was about time she stood up for herself.

"Is there someplace we can talk?"

"Sure, sweetheart," he said, lowering his hand to her back. "Dorothy, no calls, please."

"Of course, Mr. Boone."

He guided her down the hall to his office. It was a sprawling ground-floor room with a wet bar, a massive desk and a suede sofa. There were photos of the Boone family when they were younger, black-and-white photos of his ancestors and awards and company logos on the wall. A bronze bust of his great-great-grandfather

Tobias Boone occupied a stand in the corner of the room. She'd seen photos of that bust in various Boone holdings around town.

The austere room didn't seem to suit Risk, or at least that was the impression she got.

"This is a nice surprise," he said, taking her hands and tugging her into his arms. He kissed her lightly on the lips, and she immediately pulled away.

He frowned. "April, what's going on?"

"I got a *nice* surprise this morning, too. Shannon stopped by the office. Did you tell her you weren't going to buy the lodge for the company?"

"What?"

"You heard me." She gave him the point of her chin.

"I'm not sure I did."

"Did you tell Shannon you had no intention of buying the property?"

He blinked several times, unable to mask his irritation. "Hell, no. I wouldn't confide in her about that. All I said to her was that I've got a lot on my mind lately with Founder's Day tomorrow and all. I can't make a decision without discussing it with my brothers. It's none of her business, and I told her that, too, as gently as I could."

April's temper cooled a bit. "So, you haven't made a decision yet?"

He shook his head, his eyes softening on her. "No. And when I do, you'll be the first to know. You're gonna have to trust me, April."

That was just it. She didn't know if she could truly trust him. Even though Shannon stretched the truth as far as it would go, April had believed her instead of giving Risk the benefit of the doubt. Despite his claims to the contrary, Risk might still have feelings for Shannon. Just a little while ago, she would've said the two deserved each other, but now she was torn, her emotions all mixed up.

Risk gazed deep into her eyes. "And for the record, I missed you like crazy last night."

Her heart melted a little bit. She'd missed him, too.

But somehow those words wouldn't come.

The next afternoon, April, Clovie and Jenna stood on the sidelines of the Boone Springs High School football field, where hundreds of families had gathered for the Founder's Day festivities. Carnival games were set up in each end zone, everything from ping-pong toss to balloon darts.

Risk, Mason and Luke all took turns at a podium set up on the fifty-yard line, urging everyone to enjoy the day.

Sizzling-hot grills were filled with burgers and chicken and ribs from vendors who'd donated to the celebration. People lined up for soft-serve ice cream and cupcakes provided by Katie's Kupcakes. There was a sense of community and pride everywhere you looked.

April watched Risk and his brothers interact with the kids running relay races. Every once in a while, he'd look her way, and their eyes would meet. There was no doubt she had strong feelings for him, but she was taking it slowly. Their official charade would be over tonight after the Founder's Day Gala and so far Risk hadn't mentioned ending their relationship or continuing with it. Both notions made her queasy.

"C'mon, April. Let's grab some junk food before your fiancé whisks you away," Clovie said.

"He won't. He knows I want to spend time with you guys today."

"That's right, you two have a hot date tonight."

"Yeah, and I can't wait for you to get all blinged up," Jenna said. "Once Risk sees you in that gorgeous dress, it'll be like, *Shannon who*?"

"Shh." April lowered her voice, looking around. "You never know who's listening."

Clovie rolled her eyes. "At least Shannon's not here. This isn't her thing, I presume."

"I wouldn't think so." April was glad about that. One less bullet to dodge, since there were plenty of journalists here today reporting on the hundred-year-old town and the Boone legacy.

"So what'll it be, girls?" Jenna asked. "Ice cream, cupcakes or caramel apples?"

"Ice cream," April said, and the others agreed.

As they walked across the field to the ice cream stand, Risk sidled up next to her, keeping stride. "How's it going, ladies?"

He spoke to all of them, but April felt his presence surround her, his overwhelming appeal kicking her in the gut. He seemed carefree, letting loose, his smile a thousand megawatts strong. He wore his jeans well, and a white T-shirt hugged his chest and biceps. His hair was wild from racing with the kids, dark strands falling into his eyes. He was breathtaking. Masculine. Sexy.

"We're having fun," Clovie said.

"We're going for ice cream and then maybe a cupcake," Jenna said. "You know, health food."

Risk chuckled, white teeth flashing in contrast with his tan skin. Even Jenna, who had not been Risk's biggest fan, was affected, judging by her friend's big smile. "That's what the day is all about."

Then he turned to her. "April, can I steal you for a few seconds?"

Her friends nodded. "We'll meet up with you in a few. I'll get your favorite," Clovie said, and April held back as her friends got in line for ice cream.

"Hi," he said, putting his hands in his back pockets. He looked like rodeo Risk now, disheveled and, well, comfortable.

"Hi."

He smiled, and she smiled back, her heart racing a hundred miles an hour.

"I, uh, just wanted to let you know, I'll pick you up at seven tonight."

"Okay. Are you excited? It's a big deal for your family and all."

His lips twitched. "Fact is, I'm looking forward to being with you, April." The sincerity in his voice nearly did her in.

"M-me, too."

"Oh yeah?" Then he leaned in and planted a delicious kiss on her mouth. One she wouldn't shy away from, one she'd been craving. As much as she wanted to spend time with her friends, she missed him. For the first time since this charade had started, she didn't mind him showing her affection in public. He dazzled her with that kiss. After he walked off, she watched him until he vanished into the crowd.

"Wow," Clovie said, handing her a chocolate chunk brownie ice cream cone as she and Jenna returned. "You are in freakin' love with him, April."

"Totally," Jenna said. "I mean, I get it. He is pretty dreamy."

April sighed and took a bite of her ice cream.

Her favorite flavor didn't taste nearly as good as Risk had, but then, chocolate chunk brownie ice cream would never disappoint her. And she had to remember that.

That evening, April walked into the Baron Hotel ballroom on Risk's arm, wearing a floor-length sapphire-blue gown. The dress was simple and elegant, showcasing her curves. She was a little self-conscious at how low the folds of material draped in the back, but Jenna had convinced her this was the perfect dress for her, and the shade made her sky-blue eyes really pop. She'd also tamed her curls a bit, giving her more of a sophisticated look.

Risk, in an ink-black tux and newly grown beard, gave new meaning to dangerous and gorgeous.

Luke, Mason, Drea, Lottie and Drew were already at the long head table. His family greeted them with smiles and hugs, and the warmth in their eyes hit home. They welcomed her as if she was really part of the family. Her stomach twisted up tight; she was on shaky ground. She had no idea what would happen after tonight. This was her last official duty as Risk's fake fiancée.

She put her sequined clutch down and looked around the ballroom filled with a hundred and fifty of the most prominent people in Boone Springs: landowners, ranchers, bankers and businessmen and women. They were all here because Tobias Boone had a vision. He'd developed that vision into a town that had grown and prospered. Now the Boones were not merely wealthy, but a source of inspiration to the folks who lived here.

"Mr. Boone, can we have a few photos of you with your new fiancée?" a reporter asked. Gosh, didn't they have enough already? April had been photographed more these past ten days than she had in her entire lifetime.

"Sure," Risk said, snaking his arm around her back, the heat of his hand sizzling her bare skin. April plastered on a smile and posed for the camera. Others in the room took out their cell phones and began snapping pictures of them, too.

The orchestra on stage began playing, the tunes light and easy.

"I think that's enough for now," Risk told the journalist. "It's time for a dance with this beautiful lady." Risk led her onto the dance floor. "How are you holding up?" he asked, whispering in her ear.

"About as well as can be expected."

He smiled and swung her into his arms. "It'll all be over soon."

April didn't know how to take that exactly, so she kept quiet as Risk whisked her around the dance floor, his hands firm and possessive on her back. "Have I told you how much I like you in this dress?"

"Only three times."

"The night's not over yet." He grinned, bringing her closer, pressing a little kiss to her forehead. Risk could be charming and funny and nice, and tonight he was all three.

Thirty minutes later, as dinner was being served and all the guests were seated, there was a commotion at the front doors of the ballroom. April couldn't see what was happening, but she heard Lottie sigh loudly. "Oh no."

Then a sea of paparazzi parted, and Shannon Wilkes appeared, making a grand entrance, reporters following behind her like trained puppy dogs. April could see her clearly now.

Shannon looked stunning.

She wore a slinky black off-the-shoulder gown with horizontal slits running up and down the sides of the dress, showing off creamy skin and her incredible figure. Her auburn hair was in an updo that defined chic and fabulous, a delicate tiara on top of her head catching chandelier light. Her smile dazzled as she made her way to her seat at the front of the room. Five men rose quickly, each vying to pull out her chair.

April turned her head to catch Risk's reaction. He stared at Shannon, taking a big swallow, and when the superstar spotted him, she acknowledged him with a coy smile and a little wave.

Risk gave her a nod then sipped his wine, and April got a sick feeling in the pit of her stomach.

"I don't know why you invited her," his aunt Lottie mumbled.

Risk rubbed the side of his face. "It's no big deal, Aunt Lottie."

For whom? April wanted to ask. His family surely didn't want her here. And he had to know how awkward this would be for her, having her fiancé's ex showing up on such an important day. She feared Shannon was Risk's Achilles' heel. He had trouble saying no to the woman.

"I couldn't uninvite her," he told April.

"I…guess not." Besides, April wasn't his real fiancée, so what did it matter? "And like you said, it'll all be over tonight," she said quietly.

Risk snapped his eyes to her, and she stared back at him. She was simply repeating the words he'd spoken to her earlier.

"April." Risk took her hand, and his tender touch caressed her heart. "Let's talk about this later. Right now, I'd love us to simply enjoy the evening."

There was a plea in his voice and a sincere look in his eyes. What could she do? It was his family's big night, and they were in the spotlight now. "I'm all for enjoying the evening."

He smiled and squeezed her hand. "Me, too."

After dinner, Risk took the podium welcoming everyone and thanking them for honoring Tobias Boone and the other Boones who'd come after him. He praised his ancestors, speaking a little about each one individually, and then turned his focus to the folks in the room who'd made contributions to the town by way of enterprise and service. It was a dynamic and often emotional speech that brought applause and tears and laughter.

Risk looked over toward his family table. "And now, I'd like to invite my entire family up here for a toast."

Luke took Aunt Lottie's arm and escorted her to the podium, while April hung back. But Drea approached her. "This means you, too, April."

April met Drea's eyes, silently communicating her resistance, but Drea wasn't having any of it. "The Boone fiancées are invited. If I go, you go." She smiled.

April had no choice. All eyes were on the family, so she rose from her seat. Risk met her halfway, taking her hand and bringing her to stand beside him. The entire family raised their flutes of champagne, and Risk asked the rest of the guests to join in.

"To our ancestors, our friends and neighbors, and especially our loved ones, here's to another hundred years of prosperity for Boone Springs."

Risk touched his glass to hers, and their eyes met. His were gleaming with pride. Risk had it all. He seemed genuinely happy, and that happiness rubbed off on her. She was living in the moment with Risk, not knowing what was going on inside his head, where this would lead, but he'd been right. They should enjoy the evening, and as the orchestra began playing, she went willingly into his arms.

It felt so right, so wonderful having Risk guide her along the dance floor. "It was a beautiful speech,

Risk." She was touched by his sincerity, his gratitude to the townsfolk, his strong sense of family.

"Not too mushy?"

"No, it was spoken from the heart."

"Thank you." She laid her head against his shoulder and snuggled in, her body fitting with his perfectly. She liked dancing with him this way, as if there were no one else in the room. These past few days she'd felt a shift in their relationship, a deep mutual desire, but even more, they seemed to really like each other. Considering they'd run the gamut of emotions from hatred and resentment to fury and heartache, that was saying something.

Three dances later, she was floating on cloud nine, Risk sneaking in brief kisses as they flowed to the music. Then he sighed, regret dulling his dark eyes. "I should probably mingle with the guests," he said grudgingly. "Will you join me?"

She hated to break the connection. She hated to share him with anyone, but he had a job to do tonight, and she understood that. "In a few minutes, after I use the ladies' room."

"Okay, I'll see you soon." As she moved away, he held on to her hand, his fingers brushing over hers until the contact was finally broken and they stared into each other's eyes. It was poignant and real.

And then photographers were there, catching their special moment. Risk didn't blink—he didn't seem fazed by the cameras. Had he known they were there, waiting to snap pictures? Was that the reason he'd been so attentive to her?

April made her way into the hallway and ran into Lottie and Drew. They didn't look too happy with each other. "Excuse me," she said politely.

"April, you're just the one to settle this." Drew gestured for her to come closer, and she took some tentative steps toward them.

"Please tell Lottie what a fool thing she did by chasing after that dog. She could've been killed right there on the street. And she put you in danger."

April looked at Lottie's face, which was hot with color. "I'm sorry about that," she told April.

"I'm fine, really, Lottie. No harm done." She didn't want to get in the middle of this, but Drew was blocking the way and Lottie seemed upset.

Drew sighed. "I held my tongue at your birthday celebration, but I can't keep it in any longer. When are you going to start acting your age, Lottie?"

"And when are you going to stop acting older than yours? I swear, Drew, sometimes you're no fun."

"I'm no fun because I don't want to see you get crushed on the street? What in hell were you thinking, woman?"

"Don't you dare cuss at me, Drew."

Drew's veins popped out of his neck. "Good Lord, Lottie, I wasn't cussing at you, just the stupid things you do."

Tears welled in Lottie's eyes. "Now I'm stupid."

Drew looked at April, completely at a loss. He tossed up his arms. "I give up."

With that, he turned around and walked off, leaving the two of them in the hallway.

"Stubborn man," Lottie muttered then broke down in tears.

April wrapped her arm around Lottie's shoulder and walked her to the ladies' room. "He's acting that way because he cares about you."

April grabbed tissues from the restroom countertop and sat Lottie down on a settee. "Here you go." She handed her a tissue then sat beside her. Luckily, they had the room to themselves.

Lottie dabbed at her tears, catching her breath quickly. "Sorry, I usually don't break down like that, but that man frustrates me. He's trying to change who I am."

"I know it seems that way, but remember he's a widower. He's already lost a wife, and I don't think he wants to lose you, Lottie. Maybe that's why he's reacting that way."

"We've always butted heads. Ever since we were young."

"I'd heard that. Lottie, I really think his intentions were good. I'm pretty sure he wasn't cussing at you, and I know, just by the way Drew looks at you, he doesn't think you're at all stupid."

Lottie's eyes warmed a bit, but a bittersweet expression stole over her face. "Sometimes…sometimes it's just too hard. Sometimes being with someone you care about is harder than not being with them."

April saw the wisdom in that, but she hated to see Lottie and Drew miss their chance at love.

Eleven

Risk and his brothers took turns dropping by the tables, shaking hands, making small talk. He'd spoken to Shannon briefly. After her big entrance into the ballroom, things seemed to settle down with her. The paparazzi were dismissed, and the Boone security team made sure they were off the premises.

As he made his way toward the head table via the dance floor, he searched the room, looking for signs of April. Where in hell was she? It seemed like she'd been gone a long time.

Music started playing after a short break, and someone grabbed his arm from behind. He smiled. "April, where—" But as he pivoted on the empty dance floor, he stared into Shannon's big green eyes.

"Risk, I'd love one dance with you before I leave the

party." Risk hesitated, finding several guests watching them. "I'm sure April wouldn't mind one dance."

There was a plea in her voice, hopeful expectation on her face. He couldn't refuse her without looking like a heel. "I, uh, sure thing."

Risk kept her at arm's length as they danced to a slow tune. As soon as he looked out and saw cell phone cameras flash, he knew this was a bad idea. How had things gotten so damn complicated? He had an ex and a fake fiancée keeping him on his toes tonight.

"This reminds me of old times," Shannon said, her eyes gleaming. "Remember when we went to Barbados and we danced on the beach most of the night?"

"Yeah, I remember."

"We had good times," she said, inching a bit closer.

They did, before their relationship started to crumble. Shannon had a selective memory at times, and Risk hadn't forgotten the hurt and pain of their breakup.

"That was a long time ago."

"Not that long ago, Risk." Then she gripped her stomach and scowled. "Oh no. This is not good."

They came to a stop in the middle of the crowded dance floor. "What's not good?"

"My stomach's been acting up lately. With Mama's death and all, I haven't been—" Her lips tightened, and color drained from her face. "Risk, I'm not feeling well."

"Shannon, do you want to sit down?"

She shook her head and squeezed her eyes shut. "No. I'd better go up to my room."

"I can call a doctor for you," he said, feeling her body waver. He gripped her arm to hold her upright.

"No, I think I need to lie down. I'll just go up to my suite. Thanks anyway." She gave him a small forced smile, her hand still on her stomach. "Have a good rest of the evening."

She turned from him and bumped into a woman on the dance floor, the jolt knocking Shannon off balance. Risk saw her going down and grabbed her upper arms before she fell. The woman, whom Risk recognized as the principal of Boone Springs High School, apologized immediately. "I'm so sorry. I didn't see you there, Miss Wilkes." Jodie Bridgewater's eyes filled with concern.

"It wasn't your fault, don't feel sorry. I'm uh, oh wow. My head's spinning now."

Risk held her steady. "I'll walk you to your room, Shannon."

"Not necessary," she said. "You don't need to leave your party."

"Oh, I think he should," the principal suggested, and her dance partner nodded in agreement.

Risk sighed. "You're in no shape to walk up to your room by yourself, Shannon."

She looked at him then and nodded. "Okay, maybe you're right."

Risk took her arm and slowly led her out of the ballroom. As they approached the grand staircase leading to the second floor, he stopped. "Stairs or elevator?" he asked. The elevator was located farther away around the back end of the lobby.

"I think I can manage the stairs, Risk, with you beside me."

So they climbed the stairs, Shannon leaning against him until they reached her suite. She opened the door, and Risk put his hands in his pockets. "Well, I guess this is good-night, Shannon. I hope you feel better. But if you don't, call a doctor."

"Oh, Risk. Please come in for a minute. There's something I want to tell you."

He hesitated, glancing up and down the hallway.

"It's important," she added.

He inhaled a sharp breath. "Only for a minute. I really should get back." To April. He wanted more time with her tonight. He wanted…a lot of things with April.

He stepped inside, and Shannon closed the door behind them. "Don't you want to lie down?" he asked.

"Uh, yes, a little later. Come sit with me a second." She took a seat on the sofa in the living room of the suite and waited for him.

He sat in a chair and eyed Shannon carefully. What was she up to? "How are you feeling now?"

"Better now that you're here." She smiled, and color rose in her cheeks.

"Shannon, what's going on?"

"I'm buying a place here in Boone Springs. I've, uh, made a deal with Tony Russo. He's agreed to sell me his house…our little farmhouse, Risk."

He stood up, his ears burning. "Shannon, what in the world?"

"Just listen, Risk. Mama told me time and time again, I was a fool to let you go. It took me a while, but I see that now. We belong together." She had no trouble rising from the sofa and walking straight over to him. "I miss you, Risk."

"Is that what this is all about?"

"I see you with April, and it's obvious she's not right for you. There's something up with you two, and I haven't quite figured it out yet. But I know she won't make you happy. I know when a guy is truly in love, he tells the whole world, but when you came to visit Mama before she died and then after her death, you didn't say a word about April or your engagement. That got me to thinking—"

"Shannon, you're not really sick, are you?"

She nibbled on her lip, giving him an innocent look, one he used to think was adorable. She shook her head.

"Well, you're a better actress than I thought. And for the record, April is an amazing woman. She's my fiancée, and we're completely right for each other. I love her…very much."

As soon as he said the words, it dawned on him he wasn't lying or making excuses. He really did love April. And as soon as he could, he wanted to make this fake engagement real. His feelings for her were so powerful he could hardly believe it. As much as he hated the way Shannon had lured him up here, he couldn't be angry, because now he knew exactly what he wanted.

"You can't possibly love her the way you loved me."

"Shannon," he said gently. "What we had is over. It has been for a long time. Face it and move on with your wonderful, fabulous life. I mean that."

"But, Risk, you—"

"Good night, Shannon."

Risk left her room, anxious to find the woman he loved.

April stood with Lottie at the back corner of the ballroom. They'd had a good talk in the ladies' room, yet Lottie wasn't quite ready to mingle again. She needed a few more minutes, and April didn't mind staying with her. April had helped console her after her big blowup with Drew; not that she was an expert on men, but she was a good listener and Lottie seemed to appreciate it.

From where she stood, April scanned the room looking for Risk. She missed him and couldn't wait to resume their evening. As soon as she spotted him on the dance floor, she gasped, and her heart instantly plummeted. Risk held Shannon in his arms as they danced to a love song. The two of them were a striking pair: Shannon a princess, tiara and all, and Risk looking like a roguish prince. It sure hadn't taken Risk long to replace her as his dance partner. She looked away, her pulse racing, dread entering the pit of her stomach. These awful sensations weren't new—they were the same old feelings of not being enough, of being abandoned. She was tired of allowing people to let her down. She wanted no part of it anymore.

When she regained the courage to look again, Risk and Shannon were walking out of the big ballroom double doors arm in arm. "Excuse me a second, Lottie," she said.

She strode out of the ballroom just in time to catch Risk climbing the grand staircase with Shannon, her head leaning on Risk's broad shoulders. April's whole body shook as she watched him reach the top of the staircase and head down a hallway leading to the suites.

She'd seen enough. Risk was involved with Shannon. She was still in his life, which left April with nothing more than the clock ticking away on a fake engagement.

It took her a second to realize Lottie had come up beside her. "It may not be as bad as it looks."

"It looks pretty bad, Lottie." Tears welled in April's eyes, which made her even more angry, more hurt. She didn't want to cry over Risk. Ever. Again.

"It's time for me to end this charade once and for all." Her bravado concealed the pain that was beginning to burn its way through her body. Goodness, what a fool she'd been. But it was better being a fool than a rat.

Which was what Risk Boone was being to her right now.

An hour later, Risk pounded on her door for the third time. She knew it was Risk because he was calling her name and knocking loud enough to wake the dead.

"April. Open the door. I need to talk to you."

She held a washcloth to her face, cooling her eyes that burned from the tears she'd promised herself she wouldn't shed. But as soon as she'd gotten home and undressed, her tears had flowed like an open faucet. "Please just go away, Risk."

"No. I'm not going away. Not until you hear me out. I mean it, April. I'm stubborn enough to wait all night."

She yanked the door open and faced him. Risk seemed surprised, and then relief shone in his eyes. "Thank you."

"Say what you need to say, Risk."

"You're not letting me in?"

"No." She pulled her robe tight and folded her arms around her body.

He sighed deeply. "Okay, fine. Aunt Lottie said you were very upset tonight."

"Obviously."

"Why?"

"No way, Risk. I'm not answering your questions."

He rubbed at his jaw. "If this is about Shannon, I can explain."

She rolled her eyes. "It's not about Shannon. It's about me. And what I want in life. And how I deserve to be treated."

"Okay, look, I admit I've made mistakes. And I'm sorry about that."

"It doesn't matter anymore, Risk. We're done. I owned up to my part of the bargain. You can do whatever you want now, with whomever you want. The charade is over. Thank God."

He stared at her a long time. "You don't mean that. April, what we have—"

"Is nothing." She put up her left hand and showed

him her bare finger. "I've already given Jenna back the ring." She wiggled her fingers. "See, nothing there."

"You won't even hear me out?" He gritted his teeth.

"You know, your aunt said something profound tonight. And it hit home. She said sometimes being with someone you care about is harder than not being with them. Sometimes it's just too hard. That makes a lot of sense when it comes to the two of us. Let it go, Risk. Let *me* go," she pleaded.

His jaw twitched. "Is that what you really want?"

She nodded, unable to voice the words.

Risk closed his eyes briefly, and when he reopened them, moisture pooled there. "Okay."

She was touched by the tears in his eyes, but she held firm. The two of them were not meant to be. They'd tried and failed too many times. "Goodbye, Risk."

"'Bye, April," he said quietly.

April shut the door on him, and immediately a new stream of tears began to flow down her cheeks.

Risk sat in his office, going over figures from the latest Boone acquisition. The figures weren't adding up. He'd been at it for two hours. This job wasn't for him. It never had been, and it was time he owned up to that. He wasn't a nine-to-fiver like his brothers. They poured their hearts into the business. But it never had held that kind of appeal for him.

He pushed away from his desk, giving up. He wasn't going to get any work done today anyway. It'd been three days since he'd spoken to April, three days of not hearing her voice, not seeing her sweet smile, not looking into her crystal-blue eyes.

April wouldn't take his calls, wouldn't answer his texts. She was shutting him out, and it was taking its toll on him. He couldn't concentrate on work; he was having trouble sleeping.

Deep in thought, he didn't hear Mason walk into his office. "Man, you look like hell."

He didn't have a comeback for his brother. "I know."

"April?"

He nodded. "She won't talk to me. I don't know what to do."

"You love her?"

He nodded. "More than anything."

"Have you told her?"

He shook his head. "She hasn't given me the chance. I doubt she'd believe me now. I don't think she has much faith in me."

"I think she does, or wants to. According to Aunt Lottie, April's looking about like you these days."

"Miserable?"

He nodded. "Miserable."

"Yeah?" He hurt inside thinking of April feeling bad, but that little shred of hope put a smile on his face.

His brother put a hand on his shoulder. "You're not gonna let that girl go, are you?"

"I don't want to. I can hardly think straight without her. But I can't barge in on her and demand that she love me back."

"Maybe you don't have to. Maybe you can find a way for her to come to you. That's what I did with

Drea, and it worked. Remember? She was leaving town and I had to think fast on my feet. I couldn't bear the thought of her leaving Boone Springs and me."

"Drew helped you with that."

"He led her to me and believe me, she wasn't happy about it. I hijacked her to get her to hear me out. It took some convincing on my part, but it was well worth it."

Risk scratched his head. "I don't know. How am I supposed to make April come to me? She won't answer my calls."

"Think outside the box, Risk. You're a smart guy— you'll come up with something."

April rushed into her office at half past ten, her body achy, her head fuzzy. "Clovie, I'm so sorry I'm late. Thanks for holding down the fort. You're the best."

Clovie gave her a sympathetic smile. "It's no problem. Didn't get any sleep again last night?"

She shook her head. "I think I finally dozed off at five this morning."

"Your internal clock is out of whack."

"It's like I have jet lag." She shook her head to clear out the fuzz.

"More like you have Risk lag."

April sighed. "I don't want to talk about him, Clovie." Every time she thought about Risk, her stomach would ache, her head would hurt. He'd been good about letting her go that night, but ever since then, he'd called her five times a day, texting her just as often. Yesterday, all of that stopped after Risk called Clovie, giving her the news that he wasn't interested in the lodge after all. He didn't think it was a good fit for the family business. He'd wanted to speak to April in person, but she hadn't been ready for that.

So the deal was dead.

Had Risk finally given up on her? She should be glad he wasn't calling her, wasn't making her doubt her decision about him, because a big part of her was still devastated at the way things had ended with him.

"Right, no Risk," Clovie said. "But I do have good news for you. I just got off the phone with a couple, a Mr. and Mrs. Rivers, who are very interested in Canyon Lake Lodge. They're from Willow County, and they heard about the lodge from news reports and taking the virtual tour on our website. They'd like to view the property. I checked your calendar and made an appointment for tomorrow morning at eleven. Is that okay?"

"Is that okay? That's the best news I've had in days. If they're serious about it, I can call Mr. Hall and ask him for an extension on the listing."

"I thought it would make you happy. I mean, it's not a done deal, but the clients seemed excited about the lodge. And I know how badly we need this sale."

"It's great. Maybe we should get there earlier and check on things."

"We? Y-you want me to go with you?" Clovie rubbed her forehead.

"I'd like it if you'd come." The truth was, she'd need moral support, seeing that lodge again after what had happened between her and Risk. But Clovie didn't look too well all of a sudden. "What's wrong, Clovie?"

"I'm, uh, nothing much. Just have a little headache, and my throat feels a little dry."

"Oh no. I'm sorry. Your head is probably hurting from putting up with my moods lately, listening to me complain about everything."

"That's what friends are for, April. We only want what's best for each other, and I don't mind listening if it makes you feel better."

"Thanks, hon. That means a lot."

The next morning, April drove down the highway leading to Canyon Lake Lodge all by herself. Poor Clovie had called in sick, waking up with a sore throat and a monstrous cold. There was no way April would allow her to come. She missed Clovie's company, but she'd put on her big-girl panties this morning and bucked up.

Reaching the lodge fifteen minutes early would give her time to take one last look around before the potential clients arrived. This sale was big, and she needed it, but it didn't stop her from remembering all that had happened here. The joy and the heartache. But the sun shined bright today, the skies were clear, and it was a perfect day to paint a picture for her clients.

She sucked in a big breath and got out of her car. Ceramic pots filled with her favorite flowers, pink stargazer lilies, decorated the front porch. Dozens of flowers in every state of bloom brought new life to the entrance of the house. Where had they come from? Had the new clients brought them by? A gift from the landscapers?

The door creaked open, and she jumped back, shocked that someone else was on the grounds. She hadn't seen any other cars. Her heart began to race. The door opened wider, and she faced a man with deep-set dark eyes and a stubbly beard that made him look one hundred percent dangerous, yet he was wearing a charming smile.

"Risk, what the heck are you doing here?"

Risk winced at her tone. She didn't care; he'd scared her to death.

"April," he breathed out, looking her over from head to toe. "Man, I've missed you."

She couldn't let the sound of his voice, the tender look in his eyes, persuade her. "Risk, I have no idea why you're here, but you have to leave. I have clients coming any minute now."

She glanced down the long road, and when she turned back to him, he arched a brow, his dark gaze penetrating hers.

"I mean it, Risk, you have to go."

He kept his eyes trained on hers.

"Oh." She felt dread in the pit of her stomach. And something clicked in her head. She put two and two together. Mr. and Mrs. *Rivers*. As in River Boone, Risk's real name. What a dirty trick. She'd been set up. "There are no clients coming, are there?"

Again, he gave her a tender look and shook his head slowly.

"Clovie?" She couldn't believe her friend had set her up. Where was her loyalty? "Wait until I get back to the office. I'm going to ream her out for this."

"It's not Clovie's fault. I talked her into this. She only wants what's best for you."

April gave her head a shake. "In that case, you want me to ream you out instead?"

"It'd be better than the silent treatment you've given me."

"It was well deserved." The sight of Risk here, despite his tactics, confused her. Dressed in dark jeans, a black Western snap-down shirt and dark boots, he seemed to fit here at the lodge. He wasn't a corporate suit but a man of the land. Gosh, he looked amazing, if not tired around the eyes. Was he having trouble sleeping, too?

Her resolve starting to melt, she sighed and talked herself out of any warm feelings for Risk.

She couldn't do this again. She couldn't let her feelings for him persuade her to change her mind. How many times would Risk burn her?

"I'm going," she said. She turned her back on him and began walking to her car.

"I thought you really needed this sale," Risk called out.

She stopped and pivoted around. "I got your message, Risk. You're not going to buy the lodge. Enough said."

He climbed down the steps and strode over to her. "What if I said that's not entirely true?"

His eyes were glowing now, the dark rims light and bright. "I don't understand."

"I didn't, either, April. Not until a few days ago. There's been something missing in my life, something that I couldn't put my finger on. And it took losing you to see clearly, to see what was staring me right in the face."

"What's that?" she asked quietly, mesmerized by the soft ray of hope in his eyes.

"This lodge is my calling. I have always loved a challenge, always sought something that I could accomplish that really excited me. I'm not buying the lodge for the company, I'm buying it for myself, April. It's a private venture. I want to run this place, open it up to fishing, boating and horseback riding. I want to make it a destination for the adventurous guest. I know horses, so I can do trail rides and teach roping and riding as well. I'll be sinking my own money into this."

"Really, this is what you want?" she said, nibbling on her lip.

"Yes, it's what I want. But I want something else even more. You, April. I can't imagine living my life without you in it." He took her hand, capturing her attention with the warmth in his eyes. "You're what's also been missing in my life, sweetheart."

"Because I'm a challenge?"

He laughed. "Because I love you with all of my heart. I've never loved this strong before. I've never been so sure of anything. We belong together."

April was floored. She was all set to walk away from Risk, to try to pick up the pieces of her life and move on, but that was never what she'd really wanted.

What she'd wanted for the longest time was the man standing in front of her. Not the celebrity, not the wealthy rancher, but the man behind all that. The kind, sweet man she knew him to be, deep down. "What about Shannon?" she had to ask.

"I pretty much told her to go home, that there was nothing for her in Boone Springs. We are over and have been for a long time, April. That's what I told her the night of the Founder's Day party. She's not going to buy the farmhouse. I went to see Tony Russo and learned the only reason he'd agreed to sell to her was because he'd recently lost his job."

"I didn't know that. I didn't know any of this, Risk."

"I offered Tony a job. Their family will be okay now."

April's eyes teared up. "That was sweet of you."

"Excuse me, did I hear you say I'm sweet?"

"I did," she said, lifting her hand to caress his stubbly cheek. "I love you, too, Risk."

He moved her hand to his mouth and kissed her palm. "I love you, April. You're the perfect girl for me. I swear, I'll never let you down." He tugged her into the lodge, and she stared at the most beautiful array of pink stargazer lilies she'd ever seen. They decorated every nook and cranny, every table, and adorned the steps leading up the staircase.

"It's beautiful, Risk. You remembered my favorite flowers."

"Of course. I pay attention when it comes to you." And then he grinned. "And our fake-fiancée list really helped."

She laughed as he guided her to the master suite. When they got there, she gazed at the embers burning in the fireplace, the silver bucket of champagne and two crystal flutes set out on a tray on the bed. This was a special place to her. She couldn't believe she was here with him and he was professing his love to her.

She turned to Risk with tears in her eyes.

"Don't cry, sweetheart."

He cradled her in his arms, his shoulders big and broad and safe.

And then he pulled away and knelt on bended knee.

Her hands went to her mouth, her gaze on the black velvet box Risk was opening. Inside was a shining square-cut diamond ring mounted on a pedestal of smaller diamonds.

"April," he began, "you've worn an engagement ring before, but it was all pretend. And the more time I spent with you, the more our fake engagement began to feel real. It scared me at first, because I was always the guy who wasn't going to get serious with a woman again. But then something changed, something shifted, and I realized that my fake fiancée was the love of my life. Maybe we've done this a little backward, but there's nothing backward about the way I feel about you. I'm crazy about you, and I promise to love you forever and ever. Will you do me the honor of becoming my wife?"

April's legs wobbled as she bent on both knees to meet him on the floor. "Yes, Risk. I'll be your wife, your partner and whatever else comes along."

She cupped his face and kissed him then, giving him her whole heart, no longer holding back, no longer worried about being hurt by him.

She trusted him.

And it was wonderfully liberating to finally admit her feelings, knowing they were returned.

When the kiss ended, Risk took her hand and placed the stunning ring on her finger. It sealed their love, and her heart soared.

"Thank you, April."

"For what, my love?"

"For helping me find my real place in life."

"The lodge?"

He shook his head and kissed her lips. "Loving you."

* * * * *

As the Boone brothers fall one by one,
make sure not to miss Lucas Boone's story
by USA TODAY *bestselling author*
Charlene Sands

Available February 2020
exclusively from Harlequin Desire!

*Developer Tate Duncan has a family he never knew,
and only the sympathy and sexiness of yoga instructor
Hayden Green offers escape. So he entices her into
spending Christmas with him as he meets his birth
parents…posing as his fiancée! But when they give in to
dangerously real attraction, their ruse—and the secrets
they've been keeping—could implode!*

Read on for a sneak peek of
Christmas Seduction
by Jessica Lemmon.

"I don't believe you want to talk about yoga." She lifted
dark, inquisitive eyebrows. "You look like you have
something interesting to talk about."

The pull toward her was real and raw—the realest thing
he'd felt in a while.

"I didn't plan on talking about it…" he admitted, but she
must have heard the ellipsis at the end of that sentence.

She tilted her head, a sage interested in whatever he
said next. Wavy dark brown hair surrounded a cherubic
heart-shaped face, her deep brown eyes at once tender
and inviting. How had he not noticed before? She was
alarmingly beautiful.

"I'm sorry." Her palm landed on his forearm. "I'm
prying. You don't have to say anything."

"There are aspects of my life I was certain of a month
and a half ago," he said, idly stroking her hand with his

thumb. "I was certain that my parents' names were William and Marion Duncan." He offered a sad smile as Hayden's eyebrows dipped in confusion. "I suppose they technically still are my parents, but they're also not. I'm adopted."

Her plush mouth pulled into a soft frown, but she didn't interrupt.

"I recently learned that the agency—" or more accurately, the kidnappers "—lied about my birth parents. Turns out they're alive. And I have a brother." He paused before clarifying, "A twin brother."

Hayden's lashes fluttered. "Wow."

"Fraternal, but he's a good-looking bastard. I just need… I need…" Dropping his head in his hands, he trailed off, muttering to the floor, "Christ, I have no idea what I need."

He felt the couch shift and dip, and then Hayden's hand was on his back, moving in comforting circles.

"I've had my share of family drama, trust me. But nothing like what you're going through. It's okay for you to feel unsure. Lost."

He faced her. This close, he could smell her soft lavender perfume and see the gold flecks in her dark eyes. He hadn't planned on coming here, or on sitting on her couch and spilling his heart out. He and Hayden were friendly, not friends. But her comforting touch on his back, the way her words seemed to soothe the recently broken part of him…

Maybe what Tate needed was her.

What will happen when Tate brings Hayden home for Christmas?

Find out in Christmas Seduction *by Jessica Lemmon. Available October 2019 wherever Harlequin® Desire books and ebooks are sold.*

www.Harlequin.com

HDEXP0919

Love Harlequin romance?

DISCOVER.

Be the first to find out about promotions, news and exclusive content!

f Facebook.com/HarlequinBooks

Twitter.com/HarlequinBooks

Instagram.com/HarlequinBooks

Pinterest.com/HarlequinBooks

ReaderService.com

EXPLORE.

Sign up for the Harlequin e-newsletter and download a free book from any series at **TryHarlequin.com.**

CONNECT.

Join our Harlequin community to share your thoughts and connect with other romance readers! **Facebook.com/groups/HarlequinConnection**

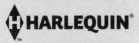

ROMANCE WHEN YOU NEED IT

THE WORLD IS BETTER WITH

Romance

Harlequin has everything from contemporary, passionate and heartwarming to suspenseful and inspirational stories.

Whatever your mood,
we have a romance just for you!

Connect with us to find your next great read, special offers and more.

f /HarlequinBooks

🐦 @HarlequinBooks

www.HarlequinBlog.com

www.Harlequin.com/Newsletters

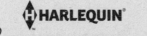

⬥ HARLEQUIN®

A *Romance* FOR EVERY MOOD™

www.Harlequin.com